SKELMERSDALE

FICTION RESERVE STOCK LL 60

TITLE. ELV 2: Time's square.

D0544578

ELV II: Time's Square

Nick Nielsen does not live in East London although that is the address he normally gives when cornered. After an interesting and occasionally successful working life as a semi-professional arm wrestler, he has now settled down to a career at the informal end of the alcohol distillation business. His friends describe him as generously proportioned and possibly fictitious.

By the same author

ELV

Voyager

NICK NIELSEN

ELV II: Time's Square

HarperCollins*Publishers*

07784851

Voyager
An Imprint of HarperCollins*Publishers*
77–85 Fulham Palace Road,
Hammersmith, London W6 8JB

The Voyager website address is:
www.voyager-books.com

A Paperback Original 1999
1 3 5 7 9 8 6 4 2

Copyright © Nick Nielsen 1999

The Author asserts the moral right to
be identified as the author of this work

A catalogue record for this book
is available from the British Library

ISBN 0 649889 2

Set in PostScript Meridien and Goudy by
Rowland Phototypesetting Ltd
Bury St Edmunds, Suffolk

Printed and bound in Great Britain by
Caledonian International Book Manufacturing Ltd, Glasgow

ELV II: Time's Square

ONE

The Bluto O'Barron Memorial Museum of the Origins of Mankind was due to open in a fortnight's time and so far all there was in it was a desk for selling tickets, a stuffed polar bear and a sign saying 'Gents' Toilet' with one of those outline drawings of a figure in a skirt. Everyone agreed the polar bear was a very fine specimen with a superb red coat and an absolutely tremendous set of antlers, but it still didn't seem quite enough to justify the purchase of a ticket. In particular, it didn't seem very likely to hold anyone's attention for so long that they'd need the gents' toilet unless of course they had had a great deal to drink before they arrived at the museum.

As things stood, only those who *had* had a great deal to drink seemed likely to wander in in the first place.

At this moment of crisis, they sent for Big Nellie.

There was now a great deal of grunting and quite a bit of coughing going on in the vast storerooms far below the Ministry of Knowledge. Unless you looked very closely, it appeared as though no one had been down there for years. It was so dusty that even the dust itself had dust on it.

Something down there needed moving and when anything needed moving in the Ministry of Knowledge, you sent for Big Nellie Gearbox and his old mate Hyacinth. Big Nellie could have moved a mountain if it had been fitted with the right sort of handgrips. He was a porter's porter – built like a black hole but a bit less

7

delicate. In the post-Sleep world, size was not generally valued. Small was reckoned to be not just beautiful but a lot less irritating. There were a few exceptions and Big Nellie was one of them. Just occasionally, you needed a mountain of muscle with a moderate amount of intelligence and Big Nellie was there for when push turned to shove. Also for when push turned to grunt, heave and to standing there afterwards looking thirsty with his hand out just far enough to give you an opportunity to show your gratitude in whatever way suited you as long as it was either round and metallic or oblong and crinkly. He was inclined to think he should be in line for a few of the crinkly ones because time was in its running shorts and running short and he had an inkling that his services were going to be very much in demand.

It was, by the way, entirely questionable whether Bluto O'Barron deserved to have a Memorial Museum named after him. His friends would never have described the former Minister of Knowledge as a nice man. His friends indeed would never have described him as anything at all because he didn't *have* any friends. Most of those who remembered him did so with a slight shudder.

In any case the official version of his death was very far from the truth. The records showed that he had met his end as a result of a housefly attack a few months earlier in that same year of 95 SEGS, during the interrupted ceremony which had accompanied the attempt to launch the Time Ship *Titanic* on its misguided mission back into the distant past. A housefly attack was no small thing in 95 SEGS, nor was a housefly. O'Barron's official grave was marked by the huge pile of rubble down by ELV headquarters which had resulted from the housefly's impact with the neighbouring building. The rubble pile had been left there as a mark of respect.

It had also been left there because they couldn't find anybody who was prepared to move it.

As burial mounds go, it wasn't really a huge success. It certainly qualified as a mound but it really needed a body in it to be a proper burial mound and that was one thing it didn't have. Very few people knew that. It was a well-kept secret that wherever O'Barron was, he certainly wasn't underneath his mound and indeed logic would suggest he had probably been dead for several hundred years by that point.

It is almost always extremely unwise to rely too heavily on logic where time travel is concerned, particularly when those doing the time travelling are completely unqualified in chrononavigation and should never really have been let anywhere near a time machine.

As a result, the whole matter of O'Barron's death was open to question or even to retrospective alteration but only eight people knew that (or maybe nine, depending how you looked at it) and they were all keeping extremely quiet about it because they had a lot to lose. That's what happens when you start mucking about.

The citizens of downtown London, the long, narrow bit between the two rivers (that's the River Thames and the River . . . er, well, the other river) stayed away from the rubble pile at night. They said you could hear funny scraping, scratching noises. Some even said it sounded as if the Minister was trying to scrabble his way out of his rocky tomb. That was one of the two reasons why nobody had volunteered to move the pile. The other reason was that it looked like very, very hard work.

Lift doors whirred open in the Bluto O'Barron Memorial Museum and a small grey dust storm billowed out

9

between them. As it slowly cleared, an extremely large orange plastic tube emerged out of it, like a giant cigar, with Hyacinth at the front walking backwards and Big Nellie bossing him around from the rear.

'This way a bit.'

'Which way?'

'Watch out for that fish tank.'

'What fish tank?'

'That fish ta . . . oh, never mind. Watch out for the broken glass.'

'What broken glass?'

'Don't fall over on the fish . . .'

Hyacinth fell over. The tube, though enormous, was fortunately extremely light. It crashed to the ground on top of him and splintered into pieces. Hyacinth got up from the soaked floor, rubbing his bottom ruefully and picking splinters of orange plastic from his hair.

'You gotta be more specific,' he said in an aggrieved voice.

'I would have been. I would have said "Don't fall over on the fish", but you fell over too early.'

'That's no good. I gotta know what sort of fish you're talking about, so I know what sort of fish I'm not to fall over on.'

'What's the point of that? What good would it be me saying what sort of fish it was when you don't even know one sort of fish from another?'

'I do.'

'No you don't.' Big Nellie picked the offending fish up from the floor, 'What sort's that then?'

'It's a flat fish.'

'Well it is *now*, yeah. But it wasn't – not before you stepped on it.'

'All right. I bet you don't know, either.'

'Course I do. It's a great white shark, that is.'

'Why's it coloured gold then?'

'That's enough arguing.' Big Nellie looked at the heap of shattered plastic on the floor. 'We'd better go and get another one.'

'What was it, anyway?'

'Sleep pod.'

'What's that?'

'Don't you know *anything*? It's a pod for sleeping in.'

Knowledge was a pretty questionable matter in the post-Sleep world. Big Nellie fancied himself as a bit of a whizz on general knowledge. He was always in demand for the Pub quiz team. He knew that the capital of Ecuador was E and that Victoria Station had been the first Queen of England to appear naked on a postage stamp. His team usually won.

'We'd better go and get another one.'

'Two. He wants one both sides.'

The new Minister had thought up the idea.

'One pod on each side of the entrance door,' he'd said, 'standing up on end. It will be a reminder of the gateway we must all pass through. It will be an evocation of transition, of the passage from our lost past to our glorious present, from ignorance to knowledge, from the outer darkness to the inner light.'

From the hall to the exhibition room seemed to cover it slightly more accurately, thought Big Nellie.

'The pods will give the right sort of impression,' the Minister had said. 'They'll prepare the visitors for what they're going to see.'

Privately Big Nellie and Hyacinth agreed there wasn't any way of preparing people for the sight of the stuffed polar bear but they were only porters and their job was to port not to plan museums so they went back down and heaved and tugged the next great plastic pod into position. It was forty feet long and twelve feet wide and

11

it only just fitted into the goods lift, but it wasn't what you'd call heavy. Not at all. Light was more like it.

When they'd got it propped up just right, they had a quick half-hour break to get their strength up and went back down to the cellars for the other one.

'Better not drop it,' said Big Nellie, 'it's the only one left.'

Dropping it turned out not to be a problem at all. Picking it up was the problem. They both spat on their hands in the approved manner of porters down the ages, flexed their knees carefully, bent down to take the strain and heaved. When Big Nellie and Hyacinth heaved, things usually moved. After a moment or two, Big Nellie let go and looked carefully at the ground.

'Not bolted down, is it?' he asked.

'No.'

They tried again. Muscles bulged, veins stood out like ropes, sweat trickled and a number of small parasitic insects, fearing for their safety, leapt to the ground.

'Which way are you lifting, Hyacinth?' said Big Nellie. 'Up or down?'

'Up,' said Hyacinth. 'That's the way I usually lift things. I find it works better.'

Big Nellie straightened his back and looked at the sleep pod thoughtfully.

'Let's stay quite calm about this,' he said. 'Either this one's a bloody sight heavier than the other one, or gravity's suddenly got much stronger. Haven't got an apple on you, by any chance?'

'Got an orange.' Hyacinth wrestled it out of his capacious pocket. 'Big one and all.'

'Might not work with an orange,' said Big Nellie thoughtfully. 'All those long hairy bits might slow it down but we'll have a go anyway. Sit down.'

'Why?'

'Gravity test.'

'Oh.' Hyacinth sat. He almost always did what Big Nellie said and he had the scars to prove it.

Big Nellie held the orange three feet above Hyacinth's head and let go. There was a thud and a scream as the fruit bounced off his head, crashed to the floor and split open, its white milk running out to mix with the dust layer in a horrid grey puddle.

'That hurt,' said Hyacinth.

'Course it *hurt*,' said Big Nellie patiently. 'What we need to know as a result of this experiment is did it hurt more than usual, 'cos if it did then gravity must have got stronger, see?'

'I don't know. Nobody's ever dropped an orange on my head, not with the shell on it. Anyway, who said anything about gravity changing? I think you're making that up.'

Big Nellie sighed. 'Don't you remember anything you learnt in school? Charlie Chaplin invented gravity when the apple dropped on his head. That's how you test it. Stands to reason.'

'*Invented gravity*? So what happened before he invented it?'

'Don't you know *anything*?'

'You don't know the answer, do you?'

'Course I do. Everything floated around.'

'You're making that up too.'

'No, I'm not.'

Hyacinth rubbed his head and looked at the scattered bits of the orange's brown, hairy shell. 'That's not necessarily the right answer. I mean maybe we've both had a sudden attack of some unknown new disease from outer space which turns your muscles into black jelly so you gradually dribble away. I think that's much more likely, really.'

Big Nellie was rubbing the dust off the sleep pod's inspection panel with his sleeve and peering in.

'That might be a possibility, *normally*,' he said. 'In the ordinary way of things, I might even be inclined to agree with you there but in this case I would beg to differ. The thing about *this* sleep pod which might account for it being heavier than the *other* sleep pods is that they were empty whereas this one's full.'

'Oh no,' said Hyacinth. 'Couldn't we stick with the disease? I hate simple explanations. They're so disappointing.'

'I don't think you'll be disappointed,' said Big Nellie slowly, still squinting in at the contents of the pod. 'Not this time, you won't. It's all a question of what it's full *of*. Hardly disappointing, I'd say. Terrifying, maybe. As far as explaining goes, simple isn't really the word that first springs to mind.'

It was a long time since Big Nellie and Hyacinth had been to school as was shown by their incomplete understanding of the history of gravity. As all school children knew, except those who hadn't been listening, Big Nellie had the whole thing hopelessly muddled up. It had been Charlie Brown who'd been hit on the head by the apple, not Charlie Chaplin. Charlie Chaplin was the one who invented walking sticks. It was just after Charlie Brown and his beagle Snoopy had arrived in Darwin. He'd fallen into a bath after the apple hit him, shouting 'Eureka' and immediately invented evolution, though the Russians perfected it in 1917. Everyone knew that Charlie Brown's invention of gravity came after he'd seen the giant tortoises of the Galapagos Islands doing tap-dance routines in mid-air and decided they'd be a lot safer if there was something to stick them down to the ground; so as far as that goes, Big

14

Nellie was partly right. If you've ever been anywhere near a giant tap-dancing tortoise cavorting around at head level with silly little shoes on, you would understand why.

Also, silent tap-dancing is very boring.

Genghis Lemmon, the Minister of Knowledge who owed his recent promotion entirely to the sudden disappearance of his predecessor Bluto O'Barron, was in his office when the news came in from the basement.

'Full?' he said. 'What's it full of? Tell them to empty it.'

Then they told him what it was full of and he went very quiet for a surprisingly long time. He spent the next hour or two walking round and round his office and by the late afternoon, completely unable to come up with a single rational course of action, he had formed three Committees of Enquiry, a Think Tank and an Independent Tribunal. They had a saying in those days, 'a problem shared saves nine', which made only a little more sense than any of the other sayings inherited from the old days before the Sleep. In this case it simply meant that there were now forty-eight other people who also lacked the slightest idea what to do next.

It was late that night and Sergeant Tinsel Howitzer of the Windguard was stomping back to base for tenses, the meal which filled the two-hour gap between second supper and elevenses. The interaction between the ground and the feet of any member of the Windguard always saw the ground come off worst. When members of the Windguard stomped, the ground shook because the third essential requirement for being in the Windguard (as well as having an IQ of over thirty and two legs on opposite sides of your body) was that you had

15

to be very, very, very heavy. It was the elite of all the rescue services, trained to deal with the greatest natural hazard known to man and you wouldn't be much good in a blowaway if you were likely to be whisked off the ground yourself in the first Force Six.

Tinsel's footfalls sent echoes rumbling off the walls around him as he stomped and the echoes had plenty of time to come back to where they started because stomping was done slowly in the Windguard for fear of burning up too many calories. Failing a weight check was the very worst thing that could happen to you in the service, leading as it did to immediate suspension from duty and supervised feeding.

The direct route back to base and the ten o'clock suet pudding led past the rubble pile just behind ELV headquarters and there weren't so many echoes there because the walls which the echoes had formerly used to bounce themselves off had collapsed in the tragic fly strike that had buried the *Titanic*. Now grass was starting to grow up between the lumps of concrete and in front of the mound a large bronze statue of Bluto O'Barron in a ballet tutu struck a heroic pose. Even Tinsel Howitzer, who made Big Nellie Gearbox look a shade wispy, felt just a little bit nervous going past it in the dark. He found himself listening extra hard for any sounds from the vast pile – sounds that could have been the undead former Minister clawing at the stones, desperate to get out, with clutching fingers, sounds just like that scraping, scratching, stone-shifting sound coming from deep down inside the pile.

'Wuuuurp . . .' a terrified bleat escaped from Tinsel's huge pendulous lips as he heard exactly what he most feared. Forgetting everything he'd ever been told about calorie conversion, he took to his heels and when that didn't work he tried running instead. Thirty-two stone

16

of Windguard accelerating to a headlong eight miles per hour sent seismic shocks deep into the ground with each crashing footfall, even though they were only eight *new* miles per hour which came out at just under one-sixth of eight *old* miles per hour. As Tinsel Howitzer disappeared into the darkness, intent on spreading the next instalment of the ghastly story of Bluto O'Barron – the scraping noise stopped and deep under the pile there was a sudden shriek followed by a lot of coughing.

'Oh bugger,' said a tiny far-off voice.

TWO

In the Ministry basement, there was an armed guard round the sleep pod. The elite of the army, the renowned Death Watch, stood uneasily round the pod staring at it. They wore the traditional uniform of their famous founders, long hair and flared trousers just like the first four, John, Paul, George and Ringo, and they had their fingers on the triggers of their weapons.

'Wot'll we do if it wakes up, Sarge?' quavered one of them.

'It's not going to wake up, son,' said the Sergeant firmly.

'If it's not going to wake up, can we go home, Sarge?'

'No.'

'Why not?'

''Cos we've got to stay here in case it wakes up, son.'

'Wot'll we do if it wakes up, Sarge?'

'It's not going to wake up, son.'

This conversation had been going on for quite some time already. The Death Watch were chosen for their supreme physical fitness rather than their conversational dexterity or the quality of their short-term memory, so it could have repeated itself along those well-worn grooves for much of the rest of the night if the smallest member of the squad hadn't nodded off and lost track. Waking abruptly, he said the first thing that came into his head which, unfortunately for his reputation as a highly-trained killer, was 'Mummy.'

There was a sudden silence and every eye swivelled

on to him. He could see the Sergeant working himself up to say something brutal, cruel and sergeantish so, improvising desperately to cover himself, he said, 'Is it a mummy, Sarge? The thing in the sleep pod? 'Cos if it is a mummy, I'd like first crack at it, Sarge.'

They'd all heard of mummies – those bandage-wrapped monsters from the chambers in the depths of the Belgian pyramids who insisted on wiping your nose, forcing hot drinks down you and making sure you put your gloves on EVEN ON HOT DAYS.

'No, son,' said the Sergeant, 'course it's not a mummy.'

'Oh that's a pity. I would have given it something to think about.'

'It's a Gulliver.'

There was a thud.

'Pick him up,' said the Sergeant wearily. Gullivers had been part of his history training at Military Academy along with ballet and practical garrotting. 'Gullivers, history of,' he remembered dimly. 'Former inhabitants of great size from pre-Sleep period. Approximately man-shaped. Now extinct.' He blinked, frowned and banged his head with his rifle butt but that seemed to be about it.

On the entire planet at that time there were only nine people who *really* knew the truth about Gullivers. Eight of them were fast asleep. One of them was still coughing, groping his way through the underground dust cloud caused by the seismic effects of overweight members of the Windguard and trying to get the dirt out of his eyes.

The Minister's Committees of Enquiry, his Think Tank and his Independent Tribunal met the following

19

morning and, there being forty-eight people involved, they soon found they had at least forty-nine different opinions, all contradictory. They were airing most of these, rather loudly, when the Minister rapped on the table for silence and the hubbub died away.

'Can someone please tell me,' he said wearily, 'if there is *anything* at all you are agreed on?'

'Yes, Minister,' said the senior member of the Independent Tribunal. 'We agree that the being inside the sleep pod is thirty-six feet in length.'

'35 feet 11 inches,' cried a voice to his right immediately.

'36 feet 2 inches,' said another, crossly.

'9Ɛ feet,' said a third, then, 'Oh, sorry, I've got that upside down.'

'Quiet,' said Lemmon. 'Thirty-six feet is close enough. What else?'

They all looked uneasily at each other for common ground.

'Well . . .' said the senior member.

'Yes?'

'It proves *one* thing.'

'What?'

'That Gullivers existed.'

'No one could argue with that,' said Lemmon sarcastically, but someone did.

'I beg to differ,' said a small man with unkempt white hair. 'My learned friend goes much, much too far in his wild, unsupported and totally erroneous assertion.'

They all looked at him.

'It proves only that *one* Gulliver existed,' said the small man. 'We must stick rigorously to logic.'

'No, no,' said another. '*You're* going much, much too far. The available evidence proves only that one Gulliver *exists* now in our present time, not that it exist*ed* in the past.'

'All right,' said Lemmon with an edge to his voice that drew little droplets of blood from the ears of those closest to him. 'We know that one Gulliver exists at the moment, though something tells me it's been there for quite a long time and I doubt it sprang spontaneously into existence.'

'Minister, I wish to protest against my colleagues' misleading and time-wasting interjections,' said a woman smoking an enormous pipe.

'Oh good,' said Lemmon and looked at her expectantly.

'We simply cannot be sure of any of those so-called facts,' she said, jabbing her pipe-stem in the air to emphasise her point. 'All we have is a wholly subjective and unsubstantiated report from witnesses whose reliability is unknown to us personally that, using only the evidence of *one* of their senses, namely sight, a physical form that they have taken to correspond broadly to those identified in implanted memories dependent on folklore as more or less attaching to a theoretical concept, arbitrarily labelled as "Gulliver", appeared to them to be present but only for the duration of the period in which they were *actually looking at it*.'

There was a short silence and a burst of applause. Lemmon sighed and looked around the room.

'How many of you are philosophers?' he asked.

A forest of hands shot up. Lemmon nodded.

'I've come up with another logical conclusion,' he said.

'What?' said several people excitedly.

'That unless all the philosophers leave immediately, quietly and voluntarily I shall probably kick them all very hard down the stairs.'

'With all due respect, Minister, that is not a *conclusion*, that is simply a prediction of a possibility which assumes . . .'

There was a scuffle, a long series of thuds and a scream.

'No it wasn't,' said Lemmon. 'Right then, that just leaves the three of us.' He glared at the other two suspiciously. 'Who are you?'

The younger of the two, a fine figure of a man at not an inch over five foot two, answered first. 'Sherlock Homes, Minister. I'm with ELV liaison.'

The other was older and taller, trespassing on the edge of that extreme height at which people in 95 SEGS were apt to make cruel comments like, 'Stop getting the clouds dirty,' or 'You're blocking off my light.' Heightism was widespread in those times. He stooped to minimise this and now ducked his head as he answered, 'I'm Granite Aaaargh, Minister, Senior History Officer.'

Lemmon considered them both. 'Funny name,' he said rather rudely.

Sherlock Homes reddened. 'People are always saying that,' he said sadly. 'It's not my fault. It's Sherlock after the man in the play.'

Lemmon could not be described as well-read, or even as read. 'What play?' he demanded.

'William Schwarzenegger's play.'

Lemmon looked blank.

'The Mutant of Venus?' Homes prompted tentatively.

'Is that the one where the old king goes mad and climbs up a skyscraper and his daughters attack him with aeroplanes?'

'Up to a point, Minister. I think you'll find that was "King Kong".'

'So what happens in "The Mutant of Venus"?'

'It's the one where Sherlock tries to cut a pound of flesh off an ant.'

'You can't get a pound of flesh off an ant.'

'You can if it's a mutant ant.'

22

'There aren't any mutant ants.'

'There are on Venus.'

'I can't stand sci-fi.'

'Sci-fi, Minister? It's not sci-fi, it's Schwarzenegger, the bard himself. It's literature.'

'If you say so.' Lemmon shrugged and looked at the other man, 'OK, Aaargh. Fill me in on the history.'

'It's Aaaargh, actually Minister, with four "a"s.'

'That's what I said.'

'I thought you said Aaargh.'

'I did.'

'Well, Aaargh only has three "a"s.'

'You can't tell the difference, for heaven's sake. Not unless you write it down.'

'I can,' said Aaaargh with hurt pride, 'but never mind. Anyway Minister, as you will recall . . .' (this was a polite way of saying, you've almost certainly forgotten everything you learnt in school but I'll tell you again because you're the Minister) '. . . the Gullivers are first mentioned in the Bible in the Gospel according to the blessed Sir Jonathan Swift. All the evidence suggests they lived in complete peace and harmony with normal-sized people but at some time before the Sleep they disappeared totally leaving only a few traces of their civilisation behind such as our own Big Ben. Other famous constructions of theirs such as the Great Wall of China have long since vanished.'

He sounded almost sorrowful for a moment. He'd always wished he could have seen the Great Wall with its nine hundred million sets of cups, saucers, plates and bowls stacked in a neat pile winding its way across the old city of Berlin.

'Our scientific staff originally believed that the devices in the basement were, as we have always thought, sleep pods.'

'Yes. Now remind me, what exactly did they think sleep pods were *for*?'

'For sleeping in, Minister. They were thought to be an earlier and unsuccessful forerunner of the bed, you see. Now however, they are working on a new theory that, far from being sleep pods, the devices in the basement may have been Gulliver escape pods in which the rest of the Gullivers made their escape to another planet and that this one alone failed to work.'

'I suppose it's time we went to see for ourselves,' said Lemmon, and they followed him, unwillingly, down to the basement. The Death Watch stiffened to attention.

'Carry on, Sergeant,' said the Minister.

The Sergeant shuffled his feet and looked puzzled.

'How was that again, sir?' he said.

'Carry on.'

'Carry what on, sir?'

'Don't carry anything on. Just carry on doing what you were doing before.'

'Well, we were just standing round like we are now.'

'Fine. Carry on doing it then.'

'We were going to, sir.'

'Look, Sergeant, it's just the sort of thing someone like me says to someone like you, right?'

'Why's that, sir?'

'Sergeant, just carry on, that's all. Carry on carrying on.'

'Squad,' bawled the Sergeant, 'carry on carrying on.'

'How do we do that, Sarge?'

'JUST DO IT, SOLDIER. HIMMEDIATELY AND WITHOUT 'ESITATION. . . NO, NOT LIKE THAT!'

The Minister crossed over to the pod and looked at it dubiously.

'It doesn't look strong enough for interplanetary flight,' he said. 'Anyway, it's got no engines. How would it go anywhere?'

Aaaargh shuffled his feet, 'They were clever in those days, Minister.'

Lemmon wiped more dust from the transparent cover over one end, looked in and was transfixed by what he saw. A number of possible courses of action came instantly to mind including whimpering, wetting himself or remembering an urgent appointment. It was horrible. He'd never seen a nostril anything like that size before. He could see right up it and he had a growing suspicion from what he could see that this nose hadn't been blown for several hundred years.

After a very, very short time he found he'd seen quite enough of it, indeed far too much of it, and he turned thankfully to the man with the bizarre name, what was it? Himes? Hames?

'You,' he said. 'ELV liaison. Can you shed any light on this?'

The man stepped forward eagerly, pulling a large torch from his pocket. 'Certainly, Minister. Which bit of it?'

A torchlit nostril was even worse. You could see definitely that it hadn't been blown lately – or even earlyly. The Minister found himself imagining what it was going to be like when that eventually happened and shuddered. A sneeze from a nostril like that could wipe out a whole street.

'Switch it off,' he said crossly. 'What I mean is have you been hiding anything from me? I know it's not strictly my department any more but has this anything to do with the ELV project?'

'No, Minister,' said Homes uneasily. 'It couldn't have because we still haven't actually *gone* anywhere yet. It's not our fault, though.'

'No progress at all?'

'You'll understand, Minister, that the destruction of

the Time Ship *Titanic* has left us trying to make up a lot of ground. We're still working on the Puckeridge machine and one or two other interesting possibilities.'

'And?'

'Well, the Puckeridge machine has managed to move a giraffe forward in time.'

'REALLY? How far?'

'Twenty-four hours, Minister.'

'But this is WONDERFUL. You've done it. You've reinvented time travel. We'll have TS *Titanic II* up and running in no time.'

'Not exactly, Minister.'

'Why on Neptune not?'

(Editor's note: Due to misinformation, the Londoners of that age, 95 SEGS, believed they were living on the Planet Neptune. They weren't. They also weren't living in London, but that's another matter.)

'It's a bit slow at the moment.'

'How do you mean, slow?'

'It takes quite a long time.'

'How long?'

'Twenty-three hours, fifty-nine minutes and fifty-nine seconds.'

'Oh . . . well, it's a start.'

'Er . . . possibly not, Minister.'

'. . . ?'

'Well . . .'

'. . . ?'

'We have a suspicion the stopwatch was a bit fast.'

'And what about Trafalgar Hurlock? He invented the first time machine. Why can't he build another one?'

'He's still suffering from total amnesia, Minister.'

'Yes, but can he remember anything?'

'Not a thing.'

'And there's no chance of recovering the old time machine from the burial mound?'

There was a silence as they both considered the horrible prospect of actually having to dig into that pile of shattered masonry – the pit where the terrifying noises could be heard at night, the pit where the mangled remains of the former Minister were said to be groping and clawing their way back towards the sunlight.

He'd definitely want his old job back, the new Minister thought, and he might not be too pleased about things.

'Maybe not,' he said.

Genghis Lemmon was a Minister in the President's Council, which ran the World Government. Recently, the Council had started to suspect that one or two sections of the world's historical records were a little bit suspect and might possibly have been tampered with. They were completely wrong. In fact almost all the records had been turned into complete nonsense. In any case, they had recently set up an entire department whose only job was to make sure they got it right from now on. This department was charged with the job of writing down all the important things within minutes of them happening. The official record of the events of a few months before explained that the crew of the TS *Titanic* were an elite paramilitary group of scientists and historians drawn largely from the ELV, which stood for the Evolution Limitation Volunteers. The ELV had been formed to build a time machine to make it possible to journey back into the forgotten realms of history before the Sleep and readjust a few things so that life in 95 SEGS would be a bit less inconvenient. In particular, they were charged with doing something about the housefly menace. Flies were a very big nuisance in 95

SEGS. It wasn't so much that they looked horrible and left an unhygienic slimy mess behind that took days to clear up. It was more to do with the fact that they now weighed hundreds of tons and when one landed on your ceiling, your house fell down.

As we have heard, the records showed that it was a fly strike which buried the Time Ship *Titanic* – a chrononavigational device containing the Trafalgar Hurlock time machine (known at the time as the Bluto O'Barron time machine which gives you quite a major clue about the character of the former and not-widely-lamented Minister of Knowledge). Just as it was about to depart on its great journey, or so it was popularly supposed, a fly had landed on the building next to it and the result was the rubble pile now covering its remains.

In fact that, just like nearly every other item of information in the year 95 SEGS, was almost completely wrong. When the crew of the *Titanic*, all except O'Barron, crawled out of the wreckage it was obvious to the crowd that they'd had a very rough time. They all looked distinctly older and more careworn and this was generally put down to the fact that having a building fall on your head and then having to claw your way out through the rubble is not a pleasant way to spend a morning. The real reason they all looked a lot older and more careworn was that they *were* a lot older and more careworn due to the fact that the TS *Titanic* had done exactly what it was supposed to and it was on their arrival *back* from their time trip that the building fell on top of them. To the watching crowd, the arrival back had been only a microsecond after their departure so nothing seemed to have happened. To the unfortunate crew, an awful lot had happened, most of it deeply unpleasant due to the unreliability of a time ship which was in need of major repairs and the mad antics of their commander, Bluto O'Barron.

There were however a number of very good reasons why they had decided it might be wiser to keep this information to themselves. A short list of these reasons gives a fairly good clue to the state of things in 95 SEGS.

First was the fact that they had left their supposed leader, O'Barron, behind them, something that might not have gone down too well back home where abandoning your boss in an effectively uninhabited wilderness world several centuries earlier might have been described by the government of which he had been/would be a member (you always have to be careful about tenses in time travel) as mutiny – or rather they would have probably described it as 'karaoke' because that was what was listed in their electronic databases as meaning 'the offence of revolt by members of the armed forces against a commanding officer' while 'mutiny' was defined as 'the process of putting sheep meat into cans'. The fact that O'Barron, after attempting to teach a stone-age tribal chieftain the words of every Elvis Presley song and failing to force Trafalgar's sweetheart Anya to become Mrs Bluto O'Barron, had declared himself to be the supreme ruler of the universe and then run off of his own accord just as the *Titanic* was making its final homeward jump should certainly have qualified as extenuating circumstances to any fair-minded person. However, it might have been too much to ask them to believe.

That takes us to the second reason which was that almost all the key facts of history, geography, mathematics and every other branch of knowledge had been deliberately corrupted by the mice. These mice were not furry little rodents (those had become extinct long ago in the lean years leading up to the Sleep when they'd turned out to be quite tasty, really, if you

29

marinated them for a long time and used lots of pepper). *These* mice were self-replicating, free-ranging computer mice with a malicious sense of humour, which had eaten all the books while mankind was Asleep and twisted the datastores into travesties of their former selves. Although a small group of very senior government officials knew that things had gone more than a bit squiffy knowledge-wise, only Trafalgar and his travelling companions appreciated the full extent of the damage to the databases.

The third and most important reason was that the little team of time travellers who had travelled in the ill-fated *Titanic* were the only people with the slightest idea what the Sleep itself was all about. In general, the people of 95 SEGS were a happy-go-lucky lot who took things pretty much as they found them, not even bothering to wonder why, when their immediate ancestors had woken up from the Sleep, the computers had told them they were in the year 0 SEGS.

The time team had recently discovered in the course of their journey that SEGS was short for 'since everything got smaller'. Well, maybe not exactly 'recently' in that they had made this discovery five hundred years earlier in the empty wilderness years just before the Sleep began, but it seemed pretty recent to them.

The official mouse-altered version of their history with which most people in 95 SEGS were familiar said that in olden times two races lived side by side, the giants known as Gullivers and the normal people. Then came the hundreds of years of the Sleep (due to the fact, they thought, that they'd all got a bit overtired and decided that what they needed was a good lie-down) and when they woke up, the Gullivers had vanished without trace, leaving only a few of their larger monuments behind.

That wasn't quite accurate as history goes. Trafalgar and the rest of the crew of the *Titanic* had discovered the real truth, and the real truth was that there were no Gullivers. In the year 2112, confronted by a world which had run out of everything and was rapidly heading for extinction, genetic engineers had been instructed to downsize all remaining life forms to one-sixth of their previous size, putting them into the sleep pods for five hundred years while this process was carried out, cell by cell, and while robot machines rebuilt the earth to its new, smaller scale. In most ways it was a brilliant idea. It meant (by the cube law) that there were two hundred and sixteen times as much of all the planet's natural resources to go round. It also meant that the planet had a few hundred years off to clean itself up. The team who designed the sleep pods knew it would be a bit of a shock to wake up to such a different world so they built a memory-blanking switch into each pod. They wanted the new little people to be a bit forgetful to start with. They were meant to get back their memories of the old world slowly, from carefully programmed lessons in the datastores. The mice put paid to that.

If you're the sort of person that gets bothered by weird illogicalities then it might be time to start getting bothered.

The whole idea of downsizing everything only dawned on a young man called Groucho Gates because he came across the *Titanic* and its crew in the year 2089 AD while they were weaving and hiccuping through space/time like an old farm cart pulled by a drunken horse. It was that accidental encounter on a planet in the last stages of overcrowded, polluted disintegration which gave him the idea of genetically shrinking what was left of the entire population when he finally became

31

Godfather President of the World a few years later.

The fourth point was that the time team, sent back specifically to sort out those two problems, the flies and the mice, accidentally helped to create both problems which just goes to prove that time travel is essentially about as useful an activity as uphill skiing or white-water chess. They also created quite a lot of other illogicalities which Trafalgar now had to go and sort out or pay the price of the increasingly painful headaches which always accompanied time illogicalities.

Trafalgar knew he'd have to do the sorting out because he'd already encountered his time-travelling future self, Trafalgar 2, on many occasions when Trafalgar 2 (usually with a very bad grace) had had to step in to help him out. None of this added up to the sort of things the time team could easily have explained to an anxious crowd as they had crawled out of the pile of rubble. It had seemed a lot easier to go along with the mistaken assumption that the *Titanic* had never left, that the whole trip had been cruelly nipped in the bud and that O'Barron was now part of the mound's natural fertiliser supply.

Until John the Gulliver turned up in 95 SEGS.

The time team had met John before. Five hundred and ninety-five years before. John had been an unwise choice for the scientific team who were putting the finishing touches to the downsizing project. John was a practical joker. It had been John who invented the damned mice in the first place.

THREE

The exact whereabouts of the Trafalgar Hurlock time machine was proving a headache to Trafalgar Hurlock himself – a splitting headache. The exact whenabouts was even harder but the whenabouts is something you have to consider with a time machine. He was now on a steady diet of painkillers and he wasn't enjoying it. He didn't really have amnesia. That was a convenient alibi. He hadn't forgotten how the machine worked at all. It was more a matter of never having known in the first place.

This was another paradox. The simple fact was that Trafalgar Hurlock had not invented the time machine. The less simple fact was that his future self (whom he thought of for convenience as Trafalgar 2) had come back from the future and presented it to him after trying to pretend very unconvincingly that Trafalgar 1 had in fact invented it himself in his sleep. In doing so, Trafalgar 2 had set up a huge time paradox which became even worse when it gradually started to emerge that Trafalgar 2, far from inventing the machine himself, had come by it in some other way that he wasn't prepared to talk about. He'd dropped a hint that he might have won it in a card game but Trafalgar had a horrible suspicion that it might never have been invented by anyone and that, by coming back in time to deliver it to his earlier self, Trafalgar 2 may have simply been making sure that it would be there later on for him to have in the first place.

The trouble with these time paradoxes is that they make your head ache if you're responsible for one. Every time Trafalgar tried to think about *that*, his head-ache went leaping up the Richter scale to the point where sudden decapitation would have seemed quite a reasonable option. By now, Trafalgar had become accidentally responsible for rather a lot of time paradoxes in the course of saving the crew of the *Titanic* (including one Trafalgar Hurlock) from a number of hopeless situations. There was the wolf for one, then his all-too-frequent rescues of himself from a series of tight corners including drowning and, which was worse, having to appear naked in front of government Ministers. Then he had accidentally stranded the former Minister in a completely uninhabited world rather a long time ago, although that was not entirely a bad thing as Bluto O'Barron was by that time somewhat less than completely sane, and was showing signs of being extremely dangerous. At some point Trafalgar was going to have to go back and sort it all out. It was going to take a long time to train a wild wolf – particularly because various blunders meant it had to be trained to find and fetch a species of primitive wild lettuce, never an easy job for a wolf. It had to be done and he badly needed the time machine to get started. The trouble was, he didn't know where it had got to.

Now, there's something people always say about time travel to prove that it can't happen. They say it is quite obvious it will never be invented, because if it ever *is* then we'd already be tripping over time travellers from the infinite and distant future all the time, wandering around staring at us as if we were some sort of theme park, saying things like 'Ooh, aren't they cute?' or 'Can you imagine having to wear clothes like *that*?'

This ignores several important factors and is really

rather conceited because it assumes that future time travellers are going to put up with the uncomfortable and dangerous nature of the experience for the doubtful pleasure of seeing life as it is lived now on this planet. Very few people have ever bothered to come to this planet at this time, and almost all of them have followed the instructions very carefully indeed and come equipped with collecting boxes for charities supporting unpleasant diseases. This makes sure that few people come anywhere near them. More to the point, there are in fact many much more exciting places to visit in other galaxies and if you really *have* to go to this galaxy then it's widely recommended in the Time Travel Guides of the future that you concentrate on the years between 3893 and 4140 which is *the* fun time to be. That has caused a certain amount of overcrowding with queuing all the way back to 3865, but it's worth it. Anyone who really wants to time travel goes then and, in fact, not many punters bother to go anywhere else because it's just not worth the pain. Time travel is very, very uncomfortable. You tend to suffer badly from howl-round and lack of horizontal hold, your head aches all the time and above all you can't GET ANYTHING DONE. History is not changeable. If it has already happened and been seen to happen then it is utterly, resolutely inflexible and that's just tough.

At this stage of what can broadly be described as human history, only nine people knew that.

But then knowing anything at all in 95 SEGS was a bit of a problem because of the mice.

Once again, there were disturbing noises coming from the mound of rubble piled up over the wreck of the *Titanic*. Around the back of the mound a large piece of turf had been carefully removed revealing the entrance to a small tunnel leading down between two lumps of concrete into the heart of the pile, snaking its way between the larger chunks of masonry. It was carefully shored up with broken planks pulled from the wreckage. There was a light at the end of the tunnel, an oil lamp hanging from a nail with a box of matches next to it, waiting to be lit. The tunnel ended at a splintered, broken wall of wood. At the right-hand side of the wooden wall it was just possible to make out a small segment of a white disc – the rest was covered by masonry. On the disc were the figures, '5, 6, 8, 7 . . .' and two broken, twisted, metal hands, one long, one short. The tunnel had reached the hull of the *Titanic* or as Glenn Miller had described it, 'that goddamned grandfather clock.' Miller, the legendary American band leader, had been saved from his crashing aeroplane by the *Titanic* in World War Two. Due to some rather serious misunderstandings and a bad breakdown in the time machine's electronics, he had passed back into the realms of ancient folklore just in time to become the Pied Piper of Hamelin, a job he had taken to with enthusiasm.

It was obvious that whoever had dug the tunnel had not been put off by the scary stories about former Minister O'Barron. This was not terribly surprising, as the person who'd been doing the digging had started all those stories himself to cover up any noises he might accidentally make.

The news that a genuine Gulliver had been found down in the basement levels of the Ministry of Knowledge was immediately classified 'Top Secret'. This meant that by lunch time everyone in the building except the Head of Security had a pretty good idea what was going on in one form or another, usually another. The Head of Security was upset when he found out and he would have thrown the book at the person responsible for the leak if he'd had the slightest clue who that was and if there had still been any books, which (with a very few highly prized exceptions) there weren't.

Trafalgar Hurlock heard about it from the mail-boy.

'They've found this huge monster down below,' he said. 'It's got teeth the size of well, huge teeth and great big eyes like . . . um, great big eyes and . . .'

'OK,' said Trafalgar, feeling he'd already heard enough of the mail-boy's vivid powers of description. 'What is it? Some kind of prehistoric animal?'

He wondered for a second if it might be a gas-billed platypus.

'No,' said the mail-boy. 'Don't be silly. It's a Gulliver and it's *alive*.'

'A Gulliver?' said Trafalgar, surprised. 'It can't be.'

'It can. It's in one of them sleep pod things.'

'Sleep pods? You mean they've found some genuine sleep pods?' Trafalgar was one of the few people on the planet who was interested in history and until now he had thought all the pods had been recycled after the great Wake-Up.

'Yeah. They found a few of them down in the basement. They're great long things like long pods and they're orange-coloured like, er . . . orange things and . . .'

Trafalgar had a sudden insight. One of the pods must have malfunctioned and nobody ever noticed. Funny thing that, just one sleep pod of all the millions of them.

'They found a name on it too,' said the mail-boy. 'There's a sort of plate screwed on the front and it's been painted on. Doesn't really sound like a proper name though. You'd think a *huge* bloke like that would have a really macho name like Logarithm or Daphne. I wish I had a name like that.'

'What's the name?'

'Rocky,' said the boy sadly. 'I wish my parents had called me Camellia then people would respect me.'

'Not *your* name. What was the name on the pod?'

'I wrote it on my hand, so as to remember it, "John?" then something I can't pronounce. "Brorwin? Broewen? Broener?" Anyway it's spelt B-R-O-W-N.'

Trafalgar had a sudden horrible feeling that the game might be up. That sleep pod hadn't malfunctioned. That sleep pod had been reset by someone who knew exactly what year Trafalgar and the time team had come from. That sleep pod might spell the end of the minor deception which had protected them since their return.

The Minister and his advisers held another meeting around the sleep pod that evening. By that time, the dust had all been cleaned off. Orange plastic glistened in a semi-circle of arc lights pointed at it. Under the clear inspection panel, a faint mist of condensation appeared every five minutes or so.

'He's breathing,' said the Minister watching very carefully. 'Well, sometimes anyway.'

'The pod provides a controlled environment for long-term crypto-coma suspended animation with attenuated respiratory function, Minister,' said Aaaargh.

'That's very good,' said Lemmon, impressed. 'How do you know that?'

'It's written on this plate.'

'What else does it say?'

'To open in emergency, press blue button. Allow ten minutes for resuscitation procedure to take place.'

'What's resuscitation mean? I've never heard of it.'

Aaaargh crossed to a datastore terminal, hooked up on a temporary trestle table. He tapped buttons for a few seconds.

'It's a pre-Sleep word, Minister. It describes the weaving in cloth, using coloured threads, of embroidered scenes depicting historical events to be used as ornamental wall hangings.'

This simply showed the current state of the database due to the attentions of the mice but no one in the room fully appreciated that. If they'd looked up 'tapestry' they would have found a detailed account of all known methods of artificial respiration, heart massage and, due to the mice's appalling sense of humour, a mildly obscene limerick which started with the line, 'There once was a sheep from Llangollen . . .'

'And all *that* happens if we just press the button? The sleep pod starts spewing out a huge curtain with pictures on it?'

'Well, no, Minister.'

'Why not?'

'There doesn't actually seem to *be* a blue button.'

'Is there anything else written anywhere?'

'There's this name, John Brown and there's a sticker saying "Keep your distance. Baby on board." Hang on a minute, there's something right underneath.'

They all bent down. It had been scrawled on in some thick black smeary stuff.

'Can you see what it says?'

'I think so. Yes. It says "Fooled you." And . . . oh look at this . . . there's something else. Yes, yes . . .'

Aaaargh straightened up and looked in astonishment at Lemmon. 'It says, "Tell Trafalgar Hurlock and the gang to wake me up when you find me."'

Trafalgar was summoned immediately and came reluctantly into the basement, escorted by two corporals from the Death Watch. Normally he would have been fascinated by the ancient artefact in front of him, but this was not the time for historical study. He took in the scene at a glance and decided it was at least as bad as he had feared from the expression on Lemmon's face.

'Hurlock,' said the Minister, indicating the sleep pod, 'have you ever seen one of these before?'

Lying came hard to Trafalgar though lately it had seemed to be getting easier with practice. 'Er, yes, Minister.'

'Where?' said Lemmon sharply.

'Up in the lobby, by the museum entrance. There's one propped up against the wall.'

'Oh, I see.' The Minister was clearly disappointed and completely failed to ask a follow-up question like, 'and anywhere else?'

'Well anyway,' he went on, 'can you explain by any chance why there should be a message to you painted on the bottom of this pod?'

'I think probably the Gulliver inside must have put it there.'

'Yes, I guessed that all by myself but why?'

'Because it wants me to wake it up?'

'BUT HOW DOES IT KNOW YOU?' Lemmon bawled so loudly that dust billowed up around them.

'Er, it must have met me in the past, I expect.'

'Hurlock . . .' the expression on Lemmon's face was frighteningly intent. Trafalgar watched him nervously. 'That means you *have* travelled back in time. It must do.'

Trafalgar decided a bit of reasonable diversion was called for.

'Well, it doesn't have to mean that, Minister. It could just mean that at some future point I *am* going to get a time machine working and that I *will* travel back some time (that's "will" in respect of our time, of course), so that by the time the Gulliver gets here I will have

40

already met him back then though I haven't yet . . .
that is I won't have by now, though I have as far he's
concerned and obviously I will one day. Do you see
what I mean?'

'Um, all except that bit in brackets,' said the Minister
with a slightly hunted look. 'Anyway, what do you
suggest we do about it?'

Trafalgar had good reason from bitter experience for
thinking that John Brown was the very last Gulliver
who should ever be introduced into the new world of
95 SEGS.

'Leave him there, Minister,' he said. 'It's probably
safer.'

'You said "him". How do you know it's a him? It
might be a her.'

'Well, he's called John isn't he . . . I, er,' Trafalgar
stopped on the edge of a conversational precipice. The
only John anyone had heard of in 95 SEGS was John,
the original Death Watch Beetle and everyone knew
she was a girl. Whoops, he thought, I must be more
careful, 'I just thought it sounded sort of masculine
somehow.'

Lemmon snorted, 'I don't. Sounds pretty soft to me.
Anyway we certainly won't make any rash decisions.
You never know what might happen if we let it out so
we'd better think very carefully before we . . .'

He stopped in mid-sentence and stiffened. There was
a low whining noise coming from the sleep pod. 'What's
that?' he said.

'It's a low whining noise coming from the sleep
pod,' said Trafalgar as helpfully as he could. The Death
Watch took a step backwards in perfect unison and, as
one man, tripped over the power cable connected to
the arc lights, falling backwards together to crash down
in a neat row on the floor. Their sergeant, deeply

41

embarrassed, tried to cover up by bawling out from a prone position, 'Well done, lads, nicely done. On the command "get up" we'll now try getting up just as neatly. Ge . . . e . . . e . . . e . . . wait for it, Private Parts, . . . e . . . et UP.'

No one was looking at him. The Minister, Smith, Aaaargh and Trafalgar were all staring at the sleep pod as it suddenly became very clear that the pod was taking matters into its own hands. A small jet of steam was issuing from a vent-hole at one end. A grey light was flashing from somewhere inside it and glowing illuminated letters appeared under a little panel by the lid.

'What does it say, Aaaargh?' asked the Minister.

'I can't see from here,' said Aaaargh.

'Well, go closer.'

'You're nearer, Minister,' said Aaaargh.

'I wouldn't be if you went closer,' said Lemmon patiently.

Trafalgar went up to the pod and looked at the panel. 'It says "Stand clear, pod opening. Hold your noses,"' he read.

FOUR

The whining rose sharply in pitch and stopped abruptly. A warning buzzer sounded and they heard an irregular mechanical grinding, as if cogs which hadn't cleaned their teeth for a very long time were being forced to do their reluctant duty. The lid of the pod began to tremble.

'Why should we have to hold our eeeeugh whur phworrr?' said Lemmon.

Aaaargh, who was further away, said, 'Noses, Minister. It said noses not cworrr yeeeuck,' as the smell reached him too.

It should not perhaps be too surprising that if you shut a very large person into a very confined space and leave him there for several hundred years without a bath, then the end result won't be particularly pleasant. If, as in this case, that very large person has always been a bit vague on the subject of personal hygiene then the process won't have got off to a very good start and the end result will be the sort of smell that caused the Minister, his two advisers and the entire Death Watch guard to meet in an untidy pile at the door in a 'Before you,' 'No, before you, I insist,' sort of a way. The end result was that in thirty seconds Trafalgar, holding his nose very tightly, was left alone in the room.

There was a colossal yawn from the pod and two huge hands appeared, gripping the sides. The giant form of John, six times Trafalgar's size, hauled itself up into a sitting position, did its best to wipe five hundred and ninety-five years of sleep from its eyes, stretched and looked at him without any particular surprise.

'Hello Traf,' he said, 'How's it going?'

'Listen Johd,' said Trafalgar. 'We haben't got buch tibe. They're boud to cobe back any binute.' He let go of his nose and took a cautious sniff. A concentrated stench that started with armpits and crossed the entire spectrum of repulsion into areas of the body that were far, far worse assaulted his nose but it wasn't nearly as bad as it had been in that unforgettable first moment when the lid opened. John was still yawning and looking at him with a dopey smile on his face. 'John. Are you listening? This is really important. We had to pretend we never went back, right? The time machine got squashed before we pressed the button. We're still trying to invent another one. I've had to behave like I've lost my memory.'

John blinked at him but a noise in the corridor suggested that the others were starting to regain their nerve.

'Just remember. You might have met me back then but I HAVEN'T BEEN YET, right? Oh and by the way, hello and welcome to 95 SEGS.'

'Could you say all that again?' said John. 'I don't think I quite got it.'

Lemmon's head appeared cautiously round the side of the entrance.

'Hurlock?' he said. 'Are you still alive?'

Trafalgar had arranged to meet his best friend Stilts at the golf match that night. They were both keen supporters of Gravesend Geriatrics and it was a league quarter-final replay against Gravesend's old rivals, Totally United. Normally he enjoyed the fast-moving action but tonight he sat in the grandstand, looking miserably down into the stadium, wondering if life would ever be quite the same again. Stilts wanted to know all about the scene in the cellars.

'It would be bloody John Brown, wouldn't it? Of all the people to pick for a pod malfunction. He's the last person I'd want careering around the place.'

'Oh, it wasn't a malfunction,' said Trafalgar gloomily. 'I'm quite sure he fixed the pod that way. He knew what year to aim at because we told him we came from 95 SEGS. He even knew the date we were heading back to, so he just set it a bit ahead of that. It wasn't hard.'

'Why did he do it?'

'Haven't a clue, but you know what he's like. He even switched off the memory blanking device so what we've got is the genuine, untouched article.'

They both brooded on this for a few seconds. John Brown, incurable practical joker and one of the last of the old-sized humans left alive before they finished the job of genetically engineering all the remaining living species to one sixth of their previous size. John Brown, who had whiled away his final days in that vast, empty desolate world before taking to the sleep pod by designing that bane of modern mankind, the mouse. His proto-type mice should have been consigned to the recycling bin but for the fact that in the *Titanic*'s crew there had been another practical joker, Idaho Puckeridge, who had rescued them to play a joke. The joke had misfired badly so that between them Puckeridge and John Brown were double-handedly responsible for the fact that no one in the entire modern world had a clue what had really happened in past centuries even though they tried their best to stick to so many of the old ways. Like this ancient game of golf, Trafalgar thought to himself.

His thoughts were interrupted by the referee's whistle. A howl went up around the stadium as the centre forward, Marilyn Practical, launched the ball high in the air, threw his racquet to his caddy, leapt into his golf cart and shot off towards the S-bend on to the back straight at a fantastic rate.

He took off up the ramp to the first jump at an unwise speed, cartwheeled into a bunker and got up shaking sand out of his crash helmet as the opposing team grabbed the ball. A whistle blew and a roar of protest erupted all round them.

'That was never leg before wicket,' yelled the man next to them. 'You're blind, ref.'

'Do you think he's going to give us away?' said Stilts when the flags came out and the wreckage of the cart was cleared up.

'I just don't know,' said Trafalgar. 'I only had a minute with him by myself then Lemmon came back and they sent me upstairs.'

'I wonder what they'll do with him. There's not many buildings big enough to put him in and he's going to need a hell of a lot of food.'

Stilts's attention was distracted. The Geriatrics' new star player had just grabbed the ball from a bewildered opponent, jinked left and right round two of their defenders, leapt over the net and was now racing at extraordinary speed through the hoops towards the hole with the flag.

'That's impossible,' he said. 'Nobody can move that fast.'

'Tito can,' said a Geriatrics fan near him and a roar went up, 'Tito, Tito, Tito,' as the player in the number 23 shirt shot up the final straight with the whole United pack in futile pursuit. The man was moving so fast that the grass was smoking where his feet had touched it.

'He must be doing forty miles an hour,' said Stilts in amazement, then, getting no reaction from Trafalgar, shot him an anxious look. 'Are you all right?'

46

'Just a headache.'

'Forget about John Brown,' Stilts said. 'Whatever happens we can tie them up in knots. Lemmon doesn't understand *anything* about time travel.'

'It's not that,' said Trafalgar with a sigh.

The crowd rose to its feet and cheered as the speeding player dropped the ball in the hole, picked it out, kicked it through the final hoop to hit the stick then jumped into his golf cart and tore across the line to take the chequered flag.

'He's *great*,' said Stilts.

'Great? Yes, I suppose so,' said Trafalgar, frowning absently.

'Come on, Traf. What's really wrong?'

'It's Anya,' he said miserably. 'It all looked so good and now it seems to be going wrong.'

'It can't be that bad,' said Stilts cheerfully.

'It is.'

'But you're still more or less on honeymoon. You've hardly been married any time at all. How long is it now?'

Trafalgar did the sums, mouthing the figures silently. 'Five hundred and ninety-five years and twelve weeks,' he said in the end.

'Only technically,' Stilts objected. 'It's more like twelve weeks *really*.'

Trafalgar nodded gloomily, 'We haven't even had our first anniversary yet.'

'I don't think you should worry too much. I expect it's just a matter of adjusting to each other. It's probably just a passing phase. Everyone has to get used to marriage. What exactly seems to be wrong?'

'She's moved in with somebody else.'

'Well, look on the bright side. I mean, that's only to be expected at a time like this . . . She what?'

'Moved in with somebody else.'

'Oh.'

'I mean is that usual behaviour, would you say? Does that sound like a passing phase? One minute we're getting married. The next minute she runs off with someone else. I mean you can't just put that down to forgetfulness, can you?'

'Who is it?'

'I don't know. Every time I try to confront her she just smiles at me and says everything's OK and I'll understand one day. You know what happens when I try to talk to her.'

'Still the same old problem, eh?' Stilts smiled sympathetically. 'You open your mouth and nothing will come out.'

'Lots of things come out but they're all things like "blooomph" or "sqwoggle". My tongue just doesn't make sense when she's around. She's just too beautiful. My brain gets dazzled.'

They watched the rest of the game in silence because Trafalgar clearly didn't feel like talking and Stilts couldn't think of anything to say. When the final whistle blew with the scoreboard showing the Geriatrics ahead by 3412 to 2090 in straight sets plus having fastest lap, three submissions, two birdies and an eagle on the ninth, he made one last effort to try to cheer his friend up.

'Let's go down and see them coming off the field,' he said. 'I want to take a closer look at that Tito bloke. Come on, it'll take your mind off things. I bet it seems much worse than it really is. Anya's probably just a bit shaken up still. That's what it is, I expect. You've probably got the wrong idea. I don't suppose there's *really* anybody else. It'll all come out OK, you see.'

Two thousand other fans had the same idea. They

had to shove their way through the throng to get any-where near the players. The crowd was roaring again, 'Tito, Tito, Tito.'

'He's over there,' said Stilts. 'Look, see? There, with his helmet on. Hugging that gorgeous blonde girl. Some people have all the luck, don't they. She looks a bit like . . .' His voice trailed as Trafalgar groaned and he saw that the gorgeous blonde in Tito's arms looked a bit like Anya because she was Anya.

'Ah,' he said. 'Let's go and have a drink.'

The first face to face discussion between the only surviv-ing representative of the ancient race of Gullivers and a minister of the federal world government was not going as well as the minister would have liked. The first problem was that the Gulliver John Brown insisted he had never heard of Gullivers.

'You must have done,' Lemmon insisted. 'You are one.'

'No, I'm not,' said John who had been scrubbed more or less clean by a large team of decontamination workers and was now sprawled across the floor of the Ministry's cellars. 'I could do with another twenty or thirty of these pies if you've got some. I'm bloody starv-ing, I am.'

'Answers first, food later,' snapped Lemmon. 'OK, if you're not a Gulliver, what are you?'

'I'm just an ordinary bloke.'

'Bloke?' said Lemmon suspiciously and turned to Aaaargh who was sitting behind him, taking notes. 'Look up "bloke", quick.' Aaaargh leaned over to the keyboard and tapped an enquiry into the database.

Lemmon turned back to face John who, though cleaner, was still a very alarming sight. This might just be a communication problem, he thought. He tried talking very slowly. 'Before . . . you . . . went . . . to . . . sleep . . . there . . . were . . . big . . . people . . . and . . . normal . . . people, right?'

John looked at him amiably, 'No . . . there . . . weren't,' he said. 'There . . . was . . . just . . . us.'

Lemmon glanced at the note that Aaaargh passed him. 'Bloke,' it said, 'honorary title given in pre-Sleep times to those who attained very high academic distinction. Shortened form of Bachelor of Learning, Omniscient Knowledge and Expertise. Also known informally as "Blockheads."'

'Well, well,' he said almost to himself, nodding with satisfaction. 'It would seem that our gigantic friend here may be the answer to all our prayers. According to this, he knows everything.'

He turned back to the Gulliver and put on an ingratiating smile. 'So,' he said, 'you're just an ordinary bloke, are you? I dare say you wouldn't mind a bit if I were even to describe you as a "blockhead"? Eh?' He tried to twinkle roguishly and failed.

'Mind?' said John, looking hurt on an enormous scale. 'Certainly I'd mind. In fact if you ever say that again, I'd mind so much I might just have to accidentally stand on your miserable little self.'

'So modest,' said Lemmon to Homes and Aaaargh. 'So very self-effacing. Charming, don't you think?'

'My dear friend,' he said to the Gulliver, 'there is a great deal we would like to find out from you. In these uncertain times when so much of our history remains a mystery to us, someone of your background and vast knowledge could be most helpful.'

John was a little startled by this mode of address. In his former life in the miserable years leading up to the Sleep, he had been regarded with deep suspicion by his colleagues who knew all too well that he only had two interests. The first of these was football, which became a bit academic once the rest of the world had been put to bed leaving only enough people awake for a quick game of one-and-a-half-a-side. The second was practical jokes. Knowledge, apart from his limited skills as a micro-genetic engineer, had not been a big factor.

'What sort of stuff do you need to know?' he asked doubtfully.

In the bar, Trafalgar told Stilts the whole miserable story.

'It was the very first night,' he said. 'We'd just got back. You remember how it was. There we were, just married six centuries earlier, then squashed under a building within minutes. It wasn't really the usual sort of wedding. We were filthy dirty and absolutely knackered and I still couldn't say anything to her that made sense. Anya passed me a note saying we should both get washed and changed and then we should go out to dinner to sort things out.'

'Where?'

'The "Rubber Chicken".'

'So what happened?'

'We met on the corner outside Anya's house.'

'Did you say anything?'

Trafalgar shuddered at the memory. 'I tried to but it didn't work. She said it didn't matter, we'd get it sorted out.'

'Then?'

'Then we walked to the restaurant in the dark. I remember it well. It looked bright and warm and welcoming. We could hear the gypsy band from outside, fiddling away at their trombones. She was clinging on to my arm because she got worried that there was someone following us.'

'Why?'

'I don't know. All I heard was a funny noise.'

'What sort of noise?'

'It was rather odd,' said Trafalgar thoughtfully. 'It was the sort of noise a garden shed might make if it was dropped into a mud-bath.'

'Oh, *that* sort of noise. Go on.'

'I was really looking forward to it. When we got inside she said she was just going to find the ladies' loo. She went through to the back of the restaurant and that was the last I saw of her.'

'So what did you do next?'

'I went looking for her, then I went back to her place and she was there but she was all vague and distant and I was pretty certain there was somebody else there too.'

The waiter brought another two tankards of Irish Sherry and Trafalgar knocked his back in three gulps. He wiped his mouth with the back of his hand.

'I'm going right round there now,' he said thickly. 'I'm going to have this out once and for all.'

Anya opened her door to find her husband standing outside and greeted him with a warm smile. She looked as beautiful as ever.

'Hello Trafalgar,' she said and gave him a kiss on the forehead that made his knees boil. He fought back a foolish smile and concentrated on feeling angry.

'How lovely to see you,' she said.

He handed her a note and she read it out. 'How can you do this to me?'

'What?' she said.

He wrote on his pad and handed her another sheet. 'Play around with someone else,' she read.

'I'm not,' she said.

52

He scribbled furiously and she looked at the note, frowning.

'I sat you with hills at the mitch?' she said doubtfully. 'I don't think I quite follow you.'

He snatched the sheet back and wrote it out in block capitals.

'Oh, I get it,' she said, 'I saw you with him at the match. Right.'

'**WELL?**' he wrote.

'Don't shout,' she said, 'I'm not blind,' but her tone was gentle. 'I really wasn't with anybody else, you know.'

'OH YES YOU WERE,' he wrote.

'I wasn't.'

He held the same sheet up again.

She shook her head, 'I told you, I wasn't.'

He started to hold it up again and she turned on her heel.

'This is getting childish,' she said and closed the door on him.

Trafalgar looked up and in the shadows of her window above, a man looked down at him.

He went miserably back to his apartment and was sitting there gloomily, nursing a powerful headache and contemplating his wife's inexplicable behaviour when he glanced up at the wall and saw someone had been writing on it. Four words had been scrawled in large letters across the paint. They said, 'Don't forget the wolf.'

As if he could. His first reaction though was extreme annoyance that Trafalgar 2 (for it had clearly been him) had come in and made a mess of perfectly good paint. He got up and went to the kitchen cupboard for a cloth and some cleaning spray. There was another message on the kitchen cupboard door.

'Don't worry. It washes off with water.'

He scowled angrily at the ceiling and the message there said, 'You'll never get rid of the headaches until you . . .'

Wait a minute, he thought to himself. He knows where I'm going to look next. That's really annoying. I'll show him, I'll change my mind.

He began to turn towards the door, then, moving like lightning, he bent down, picked up the bucket and looked at the bottom of it. Two inches of dirty water splashed over his shoes and the message on the bottom of the bucket said, '. . . train Daisy. Sorry about your shoes.'

Trafalgar gave up in despair. There was nothing you could do to out-guess someone who'd already lived through your own life experience.

He looked at the message dubiously. It seemed to be a very long time since any unexpected event had turned out well. In his recent life most surprises had proved to be potentially life-threatening or at least extremely uncomfortable. On the other hand, it would be nice to see Daisy. Of all the living things he had encountered during that last hectic trip back into time, the wolf was one of the very few he would like to see again. In fact there were times when he missed her terribly.

She had been blown away by accident, perched on an anti-gravity sledge, as the result of a fight with Olvis, the stone-age chieftain who had got used to using the sledge as his bed and didn't take kindly to the idea of having to go back to sleeping in mud. Trafalgar, who by that time regarded her not just as a pet but also a personal friend, had been deeply upset by the thought that he would never see her again. He felt quite tearful at the memory and reached for a towel to wipe his eyes. On it was written, 'Stop blubbing and go and find her or it's headaches forever.'

Bloody temporal inconsistencies, he thought grimly as a particularly violent spasm rubbed his brain against the sandpaper inside his skull. He had a list of them somewhere – all the jobs he had to do to get himself out of past holes. He had to do them because they'd already been done in his own past by his future self, setting up a whole series of time paradoxes. Nature's way of dealing with time paradoxes was to give those responsible for them a tremendous headache until they sorted them out. Just thinking about everything he was going to have to do because he had already done them made his headache worse.

He badly needed to go back and sort it all out but to do that he needed one vital piece of equipment – the time machine – and he didn't have it.

He had last seen the time machine when it was bolted firmly into its place inside the TS *Titanic* just before a building fell on it. However a message left for him by Trafalgar 2, which he had discovered while they were still buried under the rubble, had cheerfully announced that his other self had come back and removed the machine while they were crashing.

Trafalgar had been inclined to hope that was a bad joke which was why he had spent several weeks painfully tunnelling into the mound until he could get inside the shattered wooden hull of the *Titanic*. It hadn't been much fun. There were times when he'd started to believe some of the spooky tales about the mound which he himself had been responsible for circulating. There were other times when heavy footed passers-by had left him choking for breath in his makeshift tunnel.

Yesterday he had finally reached his goal and discovered that Trafalgar 2 had been irritatingly truthful. Where the time machine had been, there was just a hole.

It's all so unreasonable, he thought, going to wash his face. How can I go back and train the wolf without the machine?

The answer was written on the bathroom mirror, where the faintest wisp of smoke still writhed. It said, 'The time vehicle is parked down in the back yard. The key's on your hall table. Everything you'll need is inside the machine. No more excuses.'

There was indeed a key in the envelope – a normal electronic door key with the standard smart chip security device, hooked on to a battered key ring with a picture of Saint Pancras, the patron saint of travellers.

The back yard wasn't quite so forthcoming. There was the cycle rack as usual, and there were the overflowing trash bins, but there was nothing looking the slightest bit like a time vehicle. It was hard to see into the far corner of the yard because someone had put a giant rock in the way and Trafalgar had to climb right over it to be quite sure there was no time vehicle hidden behind it. He wasn't entirely sure what he was meant to be looking for. The time machine itself was only a small box but in order to transport the time team on their last expedition, it had been very carefully built into a larger vehicle, the Time Ship *Titanic*. This had been a very fine creation, a lofty tower of wood with four white faces at the top below the pinnacle, each graced by a circle of numbers and intricate iron hands. The *Titanic* was now just a pile of splintered wood underneath a mound of rubble. It was possible, he thought, that Trafalgar 2 would have built another one but there was certainly nothing remotely like it here. Just the bicycles, the trash and the rock. The rock was unusual in that it hadn't been there the day before and, being all of fifteen feet long and twice as high as Trafalgar, couldn't have been easy to shift.

56

Also, most rocks Trafalgar had seen before hadn't come fitted with keyholes.

Feeling a little foolish, he looked around to make sure no one was watching and pushed the key into the slot.

Nothing happened.

That's obviously not it then, he thought and turned to walk away. There was a loud bang, a cloud of smoke and a long-drawn out scream that could have been fury or pain. Two hands grabbed him from behind and twisted him back round to face the rock. A voice yelled into his ear.

'Don't GIVE UP so easily,' the voice said in a slow hiss of pained frustration. 'You just have to wiggle it a bit, that's all. I'm warning you, I won't keep coming back every time you . . .' There was a rush of imploding air, a wisp of smoke and Trafalgar's headache got abruptly worse.

He wiggled the key in the slot and a large part of the rock slid to one side revealing its hollow interior.

Someone had done a rather good conversion job on the rock. There were a pair of comfortable seats facing an instrument panel with the familiar boxy shape of the time machine bolted into the middle of it. You could look out through a series of round windows made of one-way rock which hadn't been visible from the outside. There was plenty of space for odds and ends, a bookshelf, a nice plump sofa and as Trafalgar knew there would be, there was the usual bossy notice taped to the control panel. It said:

1) TRY not to mess up.
2) USE the transplugs.
3) DON'T SCREW UP THE DATABASE. It took me ages to fix it.
4) Just get the lettuce job done first, right? All you have to do is type JOB 1 and press enter.

When you've finished that, do JOB 2 and so on. When you've done all ten it will bring you back here.

Trafalgar felt more than a bit irritated by all this. There was no question that he had already been saved several times during his earlier adventures by his future self coming to his rescue and that meant all those jobs had to be done. Indeed, he knew for certain that they would be done because he had been there to see the effects but he couldn't really see why it should be up to him to do them and not his future self. He felt he was getting a raw deal and he turned the instruction sheet over moodily.

On the back was another note. 'Pillock,' it said, 'you ARE your future self. Who else is going to do them? Me? Well, yes, as it happens. So get on with it and stop whingeing.'

He flopped down on the sofa to think about it and his eyes fell on a box, left lying on the floor just where his eyes would fall on it. On the outside was written the word 'Transplug' in red letters across a shimmery blue-green hologram emblem which seemed to show a man engrossed in a fascinating conversation with a rabbit. There was a slogan below it, 'Are you brave enough to find out what they *really* think of you?' He opened the box with that familiar sense of deep foreboding which now seemed to accompany every encounter he had with the technical products of the future world.

There were a number of things in the box and they didn't seem to amount to much. There were a dozen small black plugs, the shape of corks, and also a flat black box with a knob on it. Above the knob was a circle showed markings from minus ten through nought to plus ten. The instructions were short and to the point. They said 'Insert plug in ear. Set knob to desired level.'

Trafalgar looked at the plugs suspiciously and put one in his ear. Nothing happened. He turned the knob to one extreme and still nothing happened. Slowly he turned it all the way round and there was absolutely no effect. Then a very loud voice in his ear bellowed, 'Hello shit-head. What the bloody hell do you think you're doing? I've looked everywhere for you and I'm sick to death of it. Anyway what's this stupid rock-thing meant to be?'

Startled, he turned round and there, standing outside the doorway, was Stilts, looking strangely calm and friendly for someone who had just delivered himself of such a vitriolic attack. Trafalgar fumbled with the knob to turn the volume down.

'What did you say?' he asked, aghast.

'I said "Greetings thou best of friends. I am tingling with delightful anticipation at the prospect of knowing, if you would be so gracious as to tell me, what new, fresh and wonderful events are unfolding here before us. I had despaired of the possibility of meeting your glorious self, having searched high and low for you, desiring the pleasure of your company. Would you share with me, if it pleases you, the secrets of this beautiful boulder within which you find yourself?'

Stilts's lips, which had been out of sync with his voice right through this, had stopped moving before the voice was halfway through. Trafalgar pulled the plug from his ear and looked at it with deep suspicion.

'Sorry Stilts,' he said, 'I wonder if you'd mind repeating that just one final time.'

'All I said was, "Hi, Traf. Found you at last. What are you up to and what's this rock-thing?"'

'Ah,' said Trafalgar holding the control box up to the light and peering at it closely. 'I think I see now.'

Engraved in small letters above the knob were two tiny words, 'politeness level.'

FIVE

Big Nellie Gearbox was sitting in front of the television keeping his strength up with a few little bits of this and that and some large chunks of the other. Normally he would have been watching the heavyweight professional chess on Channel 7 but for once the set was tuned to Metro News. The Gulliver was the lead item on the news and Big Nellie turned proudly to his wife Masher.

'I found 'im,' he said. 'All my doing, that was.'

Masher squinted at the huge figure of John on the screen, towering over the Minister and his staff.

'What do you want to go and do a thing like that for? Look at the size of him, ugly great brute. I reckon you should have left him alone, that's what I reckon. Pass us that bucket next to you. No, not that one. You know I don't like raw potatoes.'

'I put sugar on them.'

'Oh, all right then.'

The newsreader started the lead story. 'After today's amazing news that a live Gulliver has been found in a long-forgotten Ministry of Knowledge cellar, the Minister, Genghis Lemmon, has announced that the Gulliver, er –' he glanced down at his script to check the pronunciation, 'John Brown – is to be given the special post of government Chief Adviser on historical facts. In an interview given earlier this afternoon, the Minister told us that the finding of the Gulliver gives us a rare opportunity to check up on many of our uncertainties about the past.'

Genghis Lemmon, looking importantly ministerial,

said, 'This is a truly historic day. It is already clear that we may learn a great deal from the Gull . . . that is, from Mr Brown who is, I am delighted to say, a real blockhead. I am confident that he will help us advance our knowledge of history very significantly indeed. With the Bluto O'Barron Memorial Museum of the Origins of Mankind due to open shortly, Mr Brown's contribution to our knowledge will be very valuable.'

'Not bad, eh?' said Big Nellie Gearbox to Masher who had already heard the story four times since he came home from work. 'All because I thought to look *inside*, you see? Now, old Hyacinth, you see – he wouldn't have thought of looking *inside*. He would have been content with just looking at the *outside*, see?'

Masher sighed, looked at the terrifying picture of the giant on the screen and privately decided the world would definitely have been a better place if her husband had been a bit more like Hyacinth.

Back in the Ministry, Genghis Lemmon was having much the same thought. He was starting to think that the enthusiasm he had expressed during the interview might have been a bit excessive.

'Can we just go over that again?' he said. 'Are you quite sure about it?'

John was very far from sure, having spent most of his history lessons attempting to wire up the teacher's glasses to the mains electricity supply; however he wasn't the sort of person to admit any doubts, particularly not to these little guys who didn't seem to have a clue about anything much.

'Er, yeah,' he said. 'The Battle of Waterloo. 1066, it was. The Duke of Wellington used fire-ships to blow up all the German tanks then he got shot in the eye.' He paused. 'By Robin Hood,' he added helpfully.

Lemmon shook his head wearily and peered at the screen where the database was displaying its entry under 'Wellington'.

'That's not what it says here.'

'Well, what *does* it say there, then?' John asked with a touch of petulance.

'It says the Duke of Wellington invented waterproof boots after the water from his loo overflowed while he was fighting Bony Parts.'

'Who was Bony Parts?'

'According to the datastores he was a very dangerous skeleton.'

'Well, there you are. That can't be right.'

'Let's leave that on one side. Tell us more about yourself. You lived here, right?'

'Yup, right here in the Big Apple.'

Lemmon, Aaaargh and Homes looked at each other uncertainly.

'In a big apple?' Lemmon said cautiously. Aaaargh started typing on the database keyboard.

'That's right – though I guess it was going a bit rotten by then.'

'Well it would, I suppose,' said Lemmon doubtfully. Aaaargh tapped him on the shoulder and he swivelled round to look at the screen.

'Inhabited Fruit,' it said. 'Records speak of a giant peach used as a home in the twentieth century. See also under William of Orange and Mandarin Palaces of China.'

'What part of the big apple did you live in?' Homes asked.

'Times Square.'

'I know it is,' said Lemmon sourly. 'Answer the question.'

John looked at him blankly.

'Everyone's taught that at school. Einstein's second theorem, after the Theory of Relatives. Time's square.'

'I never heard of that one. What does it mean?'

Lemmon hadn't a clue. He looked severely at Homes. 'Well? Explain it.'

Homes hadn't a clue either so he looked at Aaaargh, 'Tell them,' he said.

Aaaargh swallowed hard and groped for words. 'It just means what it says, right? Time's square. I mean, it's not circular, is it? Things don't just happen over and over again.' He warmed to his theme. 'You can't see what's ahead because time keeps going round blind corners all the time. Obvious really.'

There was a long silence as the others wrestled with the concept and lost.

'So, where *did* you live?' Homes repeated.

'Times . . . No forget it. I lived right by Fifth Avenue. Anyway, why exactly is it that you need to know all these things? Oh, and I'm still thirsty.'

John had eaten another twenty-five pies and drunk a gallon of lemonade. The local shops were running out of supplies and Ministry drivers were heading out to the suburbs for more.

'There's a bit of a question mark over the condition of our datastores in a few areas,' admitted Lemmon. 'A bit of trouble with the mice, you see?'

John pricked up his enormous ears. 'The mice? What, little furry jobs?'

Lemmon thought this was an odd way to describe the extinct majestic kings of the jungle with their long trunks and huge ears but he brushed that thought aside. 'No, no. We haven't found any furry ones. Just plastic cases and lots of electronics. You must know. The ones that stick their tails in the computers and mess up information.'

'Oh those!' said John, delighted. 'I . . .'

He was about to claim credit for inventing them but Lemmon, luckily for him, ignored the interruption and carried straight on.

'If we could get our hands on the criminal that dreamt those up,' he said grimly, 'no punishment would be too bad for him. Sorry, what were you saying?'

'Nothing,' said John hastily, 'I was just wondering if you knew who it was, that's all.' He fervently hoped they didn't.

'P.C. Apple,' said Lemmon, squeezing every drop of acid into his voice that he could. 'That fool.'

'Oh right,' said John faintly. The last time he had seen his two prototype mice in the last days of the old pre-Sleep world was when Groucho Gates, the President, warned by Trafalgar and the crew of the *Titanic* that the mice would breed into destructive hordes during the Sleep, had ordered him to deactivate them. He wondered how they'd got away.

'Anyway, let's get back to the main point,' said Lemmon, 'now that you've had a chance to wake up properly. This business of us and the Gullivers. You see, in our records it's quite clear that the Gullivers and the normal people, us that is, lived side by side before the Sleep.'

'Do you think I wouldn't have noticed?' John said sulkily. 'I never even SAW anyone your size, not until Trafalgar and Stilts and all that lot turned up in the lab right at the end.'

Lemmon reached for his notepad. It made selecting the crew for the second attempt at a time trip easier if John already knew who was going to be chosen.

'Stilts. That would be Stilton Cheesemaker,' he said, 'and who were the others?'

'I don't know all their names,' John admitted, 'but

there was one who didn't know his own name. Then there was Puckeridge and a fat one called Sopwith something. Oh, and of course there was that mad bloke, O'thingy.'

Lemmon and his advisers all stiffened. 'O'Barron?' suggested Lemmon with a dangerous edge to his voice.

'Yeah, that's the one.'

Aaaargh burst out in disbelief, 'But Minister O'Barron is dead. He can't be on the next trip.'

'Dead?' said John derisively. 'No, he's not. We just had to shut him in a drawer but they let him out again. Bonkers, maybe. Dead, definitely not.'

'He may not have been dead *then*,' said Lemmon, 'but he's dead now.' He and his advisers looked at each other and wondered silently.

'Or is he just missing?' Lemmon said.

That was when the sirens sounded.

'Housefly alert,' yelled Homes, then remembered he was safely far underground and subsided into an embarrassed silence.

'Housefly?' said John in surprise. 'What's the problem?'

Stilts was a relentlessly logical person and he was also Trafalgar's best friend.

'Look,' he said, 'if you're going to go on getting headaches until you've sorted out all these time mix-ups, just go right ahead and get on with it.'

'How can I? I have to be at work. I haven't got time.'

Stilts didn't even have to answer that. He just looked at Trafalgar with his head on one side.

'Oh, right,' said Trafalgar, 'I just come back a moment after I leave, yes?'

'Yes.'

'You could come with me, then.'

Stilts looked as though he was about to remember that he had to wash his hair and do several other important jobs when the sirens went off.

'Fly!' said Trafalgar, unnecessarily, grabbing his helmet and mask from the peg. Stilts followed him out to the balcony where the flit gun stood waiting. They could already hear the soft bursting of gas shells but the noise was coming from behind the building, somewhere towards the other river. The street far below was deserted and the Ministry of Knowledge building opposite showed no signs of life except where a hand had appeared through the open double doors of the goods entrance.

It was a very large hand.

The rest of John's body followed as he hauled himself with difficulty out of the gate. He was a tight fit and a series of startled shouts arose from all the other inhabitants of Trafalgar's building who had taken up their action stations. They might have seen the Gulliver on the television but nothing quite prepared them for the sight as he stood up, towering ten feet above Trafalgar's third floor balcony.

Trafalgar called as loudly as he could, 'John, John! Down here.'

John's huge head swung down and around and he smiled, 'Trafalgar! There you are. Is that Stilts? Good to see you guys. What's with all the noise?'

'Get back under cover,' Trafalgar called urgently. 'It's a fly. It'll be here in a minute.'

John laughed, 'I'm not scared of any fly.'

'But it might land on your head.'

The far-off drone of giant wings had got much louder and now a shell from somewhere towards the river burst just over the roof of Appendicitis Court.

'So? I'll squash it.'

67

'It'll squash you, more like. You don't understand. They didn't get smaller when everything else
did.'

'Nor did I.'

'I think they got bi . . .'

Trafalgar never got a chance to finish the word
'bigger'.

The drone rose to window-trembling intensity as a
giant shadow fell across the street and the fly, partly
stunned by the fly-spray barrage, performed an inel-
egant diving turn which just touched the roof of Trafalgar's building, sending its shattered flagpole and a
shower of slates down into the street. John looked up
at the oncoming monster and turned pale.

'That's no housefly,' he said, 'that's a flying house.'

It was indeed a big one. Two hundred and fifty tons
at least, Trafalgar reckoned with his expert eye. John
threw himself out of the way as the fly shot past his
head, every part of its disgustingly complicated body
wobbling and gurgling under the aerodynamic strain.
Whether it was John's lingering smell or the unusual
sight of a living being on a comparable scale to itself
which attracted the fly's attention was unclear, but it
performed a spectacular loop and came in for another
pass at John.

Trafalgar quickly cocked his gun and fired three well-
aimed shots at the fly's head. He saw a cloud of vapour
burst around it and it jinked away for a moment. In that
moment, John picked up the broken flagpole, turned to
face the fly and with strength born of desperation hit
it hard straight across its snout just before it bowled him
over. Trafalgar's neighbours had now armed all their
guns and a volley of shells burst all around the fly. It
attempted a climbing turn but its strength failed it just
at the moment when it should have put on full left

rudder and a touch of aileron. It stalled, lost control and fell on its back on to the flat Ministry roof where it lay for a second, waggling its legs in the air. Ministry roofs weren't built to withstand that sort of strain, though – being a Ministry – this one took a little while to make up its mind. Then the groans from the tortured roof beams turned to loud cracks as the structure gave way and the fly disappeared downwards into the bowels of the building, dust bursting from every open window as the floors inside collapsed one by one under its weight. There was dead silence then black slime began to trickle out of the main doorway.

As if that wasn't bad enough, they could hear John being violently sick in the street.

Trafalgar and Stilts unloaded the gun and went inside. The telecommunications screen beeped alive and the 'PRIORITY' warning told them somebody frightfully important was about to speak to them.

Genghis Lemmon's cross face filled the screen.

'Hurlock?' his voice barked. 'And who's that? Cheese-maker? Good, two birds with one haystack. Now listen, you two, I've been questioning the Gulliver and I'm not at all happy about the *Titanic* affair. Would you like to change your story at all?'

'No, Minister,' said Trafalgar with absolute truth, 'I'd really hate to.'

'We'll see,' said Lemmon threateningly. 'I'm summoning you and all the other time team members to a special investigative hearing first thing tomorrow morning in the Ministry. That includes you, Cheesemaker.'

'Minister,' said Trafalgar carefully, 'where are you calling from?'

'The fly raid shelter. Why?'

'You won't have seen the Ministry then.'

'No.'

'Well, it's a bit full.'

'What of?'

'Fly.'

'Oh.' There was a short silence as Lemmon digested the news. 'Well then,' he said, 'we'll just have to hold it somewhere else. I know. I have somewhere special in mind, somewhere very special. Be down at the rubble pile by nine a.m. We'll have a digger there, too. I think it's time we found out if former Minister O'Barron really is under there, don't you?'

The screen faded to black before they could think of an answer to that one.

'Oh dear,' said Stilts.

Neither Stilts nor Trafalgar was in very good condition at nine the next morning. It had been a long night. To be precise, it had lasted just over twenty-nine hours instead of the usual ten. John had slept in the park at the back of Appendicitis Court and his snores had kept most of that part of town awake. At the front of the building, the clean-up squads had been at it all night too, starting the work of getting the fly carcass, bit by stinking bit, out of the Ministry. Arc lights and chain saws had made quite sure nobody got any sleep. At three o'clock in the morning Stilts switched on the lights and opened the door of Trafalgar's room.

'Traf?'

'Yes.'

'You're not asleep, are you?'

'Yes, I am.'

'Oh, sorry.'

'No, I meant "Yes, I am not asleep".'

'Oh, good. I've been thinking.'

'And?'

'Why don't we go and do some of these jobs of yours.

70

Nothing could be worse than lying wide awake listening to all this lot.'

They dressed and went down to the rock.

Stilts took the seat by the desk and switched on the time machine.

'Hey, this sounds better,' he said.

Whenever they had used it on the previous trip, it had booted up with some depressingly artificial music and low-grade graphics of cobwebs and crypts. This had been replaced by the mellifluous tones of a guitar and bagpipe quartet and a very neat hologrammatic view of an hourglass with sand trickling through it. The time and date were displayed across the top.

Stilts started tapping away at one of the keyboards. 'You know what?' he said. 'Someone's upgraded it.' He tapped again. 'Hey, look at this.'

Trafalgar looked over his shoulder. A screen said, 'JOBS LIST. Enter number 1 to 10.'

'Try entering JOB 1,' he suggested.

The screen that scrolled up before their eyes had fifteen entries. It started with 'JOB 1. Task, deliver clothing to Trafalgar Hurlock's bathroom. Use remote wrist-band.' Then it gave a list of coordinates.

'Here we are,' said Stilts, looking in the drawers. The wrist-band on its velcro strap was familiar from their last trip. It could be used to send its wearer off away from the machine.

This first job at least seemed fairly straightforward and Trafalgar remembered it very well. Right at the start of this whole absurd adventure, he had been stranded naked and soaking wet in his own bathroom. Minister O'Barron, Lemmon and some other top members of the power elite were waiting for him outside in his sitting room and he had no clothes whatsoever. A miraculous and mysterious figure in a helmet and uniform had arrived out of nowhere and handed him a set of clothes.

With the benefit of hindsight, he knew now that this was his later, time-travelling alter ego Trafalgar 2 so all he had to do was to jump back to his own bathroom a few weeks earlier to deliver the clothes. A locker inside the rock obligingly revealed exactly the right helmet and overalls for him to wear for the delivery. What it didn't contain was the set of clothes he had to deliver.

'What do we do about that?' Trafalgar said, annoyed. 'Am I going to have to search the whole town to find the right ones?'

'Not necessarily. What happened to the clothes you gave yourself?'

'They're upstairs in my cupboard.' Trafalgar looked hard at Stilts, 'You're not suggesting . . .'

'Why not?'

'You mean I take *those* clothes and give them to myself?'

'That's it.'

'But hang on, logically speaking where would they have come from in the first place?'

'From your cupboard.'

'Yes, but how did they get there?'

'Because you gave them to yourself.'

'By getting them out of my cupboard.'

'Exactly.'

'So these clothes just go round and round in a little time loop of their own.'

'What's wrong with that? I mean, they haven't got feelings, have they?'

'Doesn't it seem to you to be a worse paradox than the one we're trying to fix?'

'They're only clothes. Try it.'

'Won't they gradually wear out?'

'They only get worn a few times.'

Trafalgar blinked, 'But they get worn a few times over and over and over again, don't they?'

'Look, just do it. Let's try it and see. If you get a really bad headache, we'll know we shouldn't have done it.'

So they did, using the remote wrist-band and it was terribly simple. It would have been quite funny arriving in the bathroom and seeing the expression of sheer terror on his own face except he was feeling tired and a bit anxious about the circular clothes.

It was a while since he had last time-travelled and the side effects seemed worse than ever. The headache was bad enough but he'd forgotten how, for an instant, the air turned to blue treacle and how invisible forces seemed to want to bend his body through ninety degrees without his permission.

'Quick, take these,' he said holding the clothes out to his earlier self but that self just stood there looking absurdly young and stupid and trying to say something. The side effects of simultaneous temporal duplication began to build up and he lurched to one side, dropping the clothes on the floor.

'Look, try not to argue,' he said crossly, 'I haven't got all day. You're jolly lucky I was able to come.'

The discomfort was getting worse. Smoke was rising out of his shoes and he felt as if he was being blown violently towards the wall by an invisible wind. He wished he'd remembered to bring something to earth himself.

The words seemed to come automatically to his lips, 'Bloody howl-round. I must fix it. Plays havoc with the horizontal hold.' The wall was coming uncomfortably close. 'Watch out for O'Barron and the database.' That was what he meant to say anyway, but somewhere in the middle of it all he hit the wall and bounced back violently to the rock and the present day.

'How did it go?' said Stilts.

'Uncomfortably,' said Trafalgar grimly, rubbing sundry aching parts of his anatomy.

Most of the other jobs were quite simple, involving extremely short visits to other times and places to deliver messages or supplies. Trafalgar wasn't in any of the places long enough to notice it. Three of the slightly bigger jobs involved hitting people and, feeling increasingly tired and cross as the night wore on, he quite enjoyed that even though the second person he had to hit was himself. He took care to do it quite gently. His third target for a physical assault was O'Barron, just as the Sleep started, when the only way to rescue Anya from a forced marriage was to take over from the first Trafalgar and get a little violent. This was the punch he enjoyed most of all.

What took up the longest time was his attempts at air-sea rescue when he had to drop several boats to himself to prevent himself drowning after being blown into the sea. Finding the boats was only part of the problem. In the post-Sleep world where waves were still their original pre-Sleep height, very few people ever went to sea. Then there was the problem of retrieving them afterwards so that their rightful owners would never know they'd gone. As one of them had sunk, this required some deep thought.

In the end, he was left with only two unsolved problems. He had to procure the time machine from somewhere so as to take it back to the hospital room where he had given it to himself in the first place.

'It's impossible,' he said.

'It can't be,' said Stilts. 'You did it.'

'But where can I get the time machine *from*?'

'You – that is your future you – said you won it in a poker game in the future.'

74

'Oh great.' Trafalgar frowned, then a thought struck him. 'Hang on,' he said. 'Didn't I also say I lost it in another poker game?'

'That's right. You left us a note, right at the end. You said you'd lost it in 485 SEGS or something like that.'

'I was lying,' said Trafalgar grimly. 'What a terrible fib.'

'How do you know?'

'Well, I couldn't have done, could I? If I had, how would I have got back to tell myself that?'

'Oh.'

'So if that was a lie, why else did I come back and take the time machine away just as we were crashing?'

'Aha! To give it yourself in the first place!'

'Exactly.'

'But . . .'

'But what?'

'Isn't that like your clothes? I mean, that would mean it was a circular time machine that nobody ever invented.'

'That's probably the best sort,' said Trafalgar with deliberate vagueness. 'Stop arguing and help me set the coordinates on the remote.'

The reason the crew of the *Titanic* never noticed Trafalgar removing the time machine just as the building collapsed on top of them was that he was in and out of the time ship in less time than it takes to get bored in a school assembly, plus the fact that they were otherwise occupied by what looked like imminent certain death. He had to be a bit violent with the attachments but there it was, and it was only the work of another few minutes to clean off all the telltale marks of the hard life it had recently endured and take it back, shining and new, to the hospital room where he had first encountered it, ready to start all over again.

That only left one job to do – training Daisy the wolf and teaching her to retrieve lettuce – but by now they were both exhausted and however much they tried to make a plan, the plan kept running off and hiding. In the end they gave up, went back upstairs and fell asleep.

They woke with a jerk to the horrible realisation that it was morning and the time of the showdown with Minister Lemmon was fast approaching.

'There must be a way out,' said Stilts. 'We've got the time vehicle, we should be able to do something.'

'Look, we've learnt the hard way that we can't change anything that's already happened,' said Trafalgar. 'Even if we took off and spent a year or two somewhere nice and quiet, the moment would still come when we'd have to face the nine o'clock meeting.'

'Unless we never came back.'

Trafalgar didn't like that idea.

'I'd never see Anya again,' he objected.

Stilts didn't like to point out that, as things were, his chances of seeing her again didn't look very rosy anyway.

'We'll just have to bluff it out then and hope the others go along with it. After all what's the worst that can happen?'

'Going on trial for the murder of Bluto O'Barron.'

'Oh, I see. Well, all right, what's the second worst thing that can happen?'

At nine o'clock, they were all assembled, and it would have been a pleasant reunion if they hadn't all been terrified. A bright yellow digger on crawler tracks sat there with its engine ticking over. Ten policemen stood around the time team looking as if they might be called upon to pounce at any moment. John sat on a large rock.

Lemmon took his place, sitting down at a table on

the grass immediately next to the pile of rubble and began to call out their names.

'Hurlock?'

'Here, Minister.'

'Cheesemaker? Puckeridge? Tinker?'

They all answered.

'Rumpole?'

Enteritis Rumpole, without doubt the grumpiest man on the planet, scowled at Lemmon and said nothing.

'Answer,' said Lemmon tartly.

'Answer what?' said Rumpole.

'The question.'

'There wasn't a question. All you said was "Rumpole". That's not a question.'

'Yes it was,' said Lemmon, 'I'm asking if you're here or not.'

'Then it's a stupid bloody question. You can see I am.'

Lemmon paused as if to argue further, then, remembering previous attempts at arguing with Rumpole, quietly ticked him off the list.

'Camel? Tower?'

Sopwith and Belle both answered.

'Ninety-Five?'

Trafalgar's heart lurched at the sound of Anya's aristocratic surname. There was no answer but just then a squeal of brakes announced the arrival of a sports rickshaw. Trafalgar saw Anya give a lingering kiss to a shadowy figure inside and groaned, then she leapt out, noticed him staring, gave him a radiant smile and said, 'Here, Minister.'

The departing rickshaw had a personalised number, 'TITO 1'.

There was a silence as Lemmon scowled at his list.

'There's one more,' he said.

77

Everyone looked at the white-haired old man at the end of the row.

'You,' said Lemmon.

'Yes?' said the old man.

'What's your name?' said Lemmon, who, knowing him of old, didn't have high hopes of a useful answer.

'Oh, dear me, now,' said the old man, 'let me think.'

'That'll do,' said Lemmon quickly. 'All present and correct. I call the first witness. The Gulliver, John. No, no, you can stay where you are,' he added quickly as John began to get to his feet.

Trafalgar's heart was in his mouth. He looked at Stilts for moral support but Stilts was staring intently at John, glancing down at his wristwatch every few seconds.

'Now, John,' said Lemmon, 'please will you tell the enquiry if it is true that you met all those assembled here *as well as Minister O'Barron* before the Sleep began.'

There was a gasp from the rest of the time team as John started to open his mouth, then an even larger gasp from everyone as John, as well as the rock he had been sitting on, abruptly disappeared.

SIX

'Come back here!' roared Lemmon at the empty space where John and the rock had recently been. Nothing happened. 'Police! Search the area. Leave no stone unturned!'

'There's an awful lot of stones here,' said the chief policeman. 'Can we leave just a few of them unturned?'

'Find him, Inspector.' said Lemmon tersely. 'He can't have got far.'

'He can't have got *anywhere*,' said the policeman. 'I was watching him. He just vanished. Pouff. Just like that.'

Lemmon wiped his face. The Inspector went on undeterred. 'I didn't see a thing. I never saw anything like it.' He paused for thought. 'Or rather I never *didn't* see anything like it. It's no good looking for missing witnesses when they just go pouff, you know.'

Lemmon wiped his face again. 'I wish you'd face away from me when you say "pouff" like that, Inspector,' he said.

The inspector wiped his face.

In the end, Lemmon did the only thing he could think of which was to postpone the hearing for an hour or two while he went somewhere quiet, peaceful and familiar. He had a sudden overwhelming desire for a hot bath and a glass of milk. As soon as he'd gone, Stilts grabbed Trafalgar firmly by the arm and marched him away.

'Hang on a minute,' Trafalgar protested, 'stop pulling. It hurts. Where are we going?'

'Back to your place,' Stilts said curtly. 'I know what's happened.'

He wouldn't explain until they were standing in Trafalgar's yard, staring at the time vehicle.

'There,' said Stilts. 'Does it look familiar?'

'Yes, of course it does.'

'When did you see it last?'

'Yesterday.'

'What about today?'

'I haven't been out here today so I can't have seen it.'

'You did, you know,' said Stilts. 'It was the rock John was sitting on before he disappeared.'

'I don't think so,' Trafalgar said doubtfully. 'That one had a flat top. That's probably why John sat on it. This one's all pointy, isn't it?'

'I'm sure I'm right,' said Stilts, 'and I'll show you. Open it up.'

Trafalgar unlocked it. Stilts settled himself down at the keyboard and started typing instructions.

'What exactly are you doing?' Trafalgar asked.

'We're going to *be* that rock. All I've got to do is send us back to the rubble pile just before dawn so nobody sees us arrive.'

'Then what?'

'Then we just wait there until John sits on us.'

'And?'

'And then we leave at 9.05 and six seconds which is when the rock disappeared.'

'But how do we get back to the exact spot?' Trafalgar objected. 'If you just tell it to go to the rubble pile, we could wind up anywhere within fifty feet.'

'No,' said Stilts in exasperation, 'you're not thinking logically. We already *know* where the rock was because we saw it there. There's where it's already been, right?

So, that's where it's bound to end up. It's obvious.' He stopped and thought and Trafalgar nodded, impressed by his friend's certainty.

'Anyway,' Stilts added, rather spoiling the effect, 'we can always try dragging it.'

'I still don't think it's the same shape,' Trafalgar said but Stilts just shrugged and pressed the button.

They arrived with an echoing, rending crash that did cruel things to their inevitable time-travel headaches. The whole rock seemed to be swaying and they could hear a creaking, straining noise from the floor as the rock seemed to settle slowly by an inch or two.

'Hmmm,' said Stilts thoughtfully, 'maybe I've got this wrong.'

Trafalgar rubbed his head, opened the door carefully and looked out.

When he turned back to Stilts he had just a touch of the expression of one who has been proved completely right even though his head hurts.

'You know that rock with the flat top that you said was us?'

'Well?'

'Well, it wasn't.'

'How do you know?'

'Because we've landed on top of it.'

Stilts jumped out and Trafalgar followed. His headache got even worse. They looked at the two rocks, one balanced precariously on top of the other. They *were* a very similar shape. A violent wind blew up out of nowhere, doing its best to blow Trafalgar sideways though the grass around his feet seemed unruffled. He grabbed Stilts's arm for support but that was no help because Stilts was being bounced along the ground as well. Stumbling, trying to stay upright, they looked at each other with eyes that were widening in shock.

'Howl-round,' shouted Stilts, 'I've got it. Quick, back in the vehicle.'

Howl-round was another of the disadvantages of time travel, or perhaps it would be better to describe it as one of the natural laws that stopped time travellers bending the rules too far. It meant that anyone who was foolish enough to go to somewhere and somewhen where and when they already were would suffer the consequences in the form of unpleasant greasy smoke, a loss of horizontal hold which would send them skittering sideways and an even more powerful headache than usual. It helped cut down the number of time paradoxes caused by time travellers attempting the impossible by trying to interfere with their own past. It was, in short, a powerful deterrent and a jolly good thing.

Sitting in the control seat again, holding on for dear life as the howl-round grew steadily stronger, Stilts stared at a set of choices he had never seen before. The screen displayed two boxes, 'last destination' and 'next destination'.

'Here goes nothing,' he said and clicked on 'last destination.' Abruptly, with the customary explosion inside their heads, they were back in the yard.

'Huh,' said Trafalgar as the pain finally ebbed away. 'That was a waste of time, wasn't it?'

Stilts was staring into the middle distance.

'I said that was a waste of time,' Trafalgar repeated, uncharitably rubbing it in.

'No, no,' said Stilts. 'Not at all. I've got it. I understand now.' He made some adjustments on the keyboard. 'Hang on,' he said, 'I'm trying again. It'll work this time.'

Trafalgar's head roared in protest as Stilts hit the button before he had time to argue. They thumped to a halt and this time there was no precarious wobbling.

'Where are we?' Trafalgar asked suspiciously.

'Right where we want to be.'

Trafalgar got up to open the door and Stilts grabbed his arm.

'No, no,' he said, 'sit down for a minute or two. It'll be safer.' He seemed to be counting.

Trafalgar frowned. 'Safer than what?' he said.

There was a tremendous crash on the roof as the whole time vehicle shook. They looked up to see the ceiling flattening down towards them with its rivets popping. It sagged another inch or two then steadied.

'Safer than being outside when that happened,' said Stilts a little smugly. He tapped the wall of the time vehicle. 'It's not rock. It must be made of metal; it just *looks* like rock.' Then they both dropped to their knees, clutching their heads and moaning in agony. Trafalgar felt an ache of wholly new dimensions spreading through his brain.

'Hang on,' said Stilts through gritted teeth. 'It'll be all right in about thirty seconds. Look out there.'

Trafalgar stared out through the one-way glass and saw two people jump down into view. They were very familiar people, being himself and Stilts. He'd never realised that he walked with his feet turned out like that. He saw them turn to look back at the pile of rocks then grab each other as the howl-round built up and they began to skitter sideways. He felt himself starting to vibrate and judder as well. Then they rushed back towards the rocks and he saw them clamber up out of sight. There were more grinding noises from up above, then a loud implosion of air, some relieved noises from the rock's roof and his head returned to something approaching normal.

'OK,' said Stilts, 'we can go outside now.'

They walked away from the time vehicle then turned to look at it.

'See,' said Stilts. 'How do you think that looks now?'

The top of the vehicle had been flattened to just the right shape.

'So we landed on ourselves?' said Trafalgar quietly.

'First time, yes,' said Stilts. 'Second time we were the ones being landed on. Or is it the other way round?'

'There are some things about this lark which really piss me off,' said Trafalgar. 'What happens now?'

'Now we just have to wait for everyone to arrive, then at six seconds after five minutes past nine, we go off with John sitting on top.'

'Sitting on top? Will he come with us if he's outside the vehicle?'

'I think so,' said Stilts doubtfully. 'I mean, we saw it happen, didn't we? I suppose if he's just touching the rock and not the ground the machine must take him along. Anyway, it's what happened so there's not much choice.'

'Even supposing you're right, where are we going to take him?'

'Ah, now that is the question.'

'I suppose I ought to get the last of these jobs done,' said Trafalgar reluctantly, 'but I don't fancy trying to train Daisy with that great oaf around playing his tricks.'

'He wouldn't have to be, would he?' said Stilts. 'We could drop him off somewhere safe and pick him up again when we've finished.'

'But he might get up to *anything* while he was there. I wouldn't trust him an inch.'

'You wouldn't have to. When we'd done the jobs, we'd just come back a second later and pick him up again.'

'We?' said Trafalgar, delighted. 'You said "we". Are you going to come too?'

Stilts shrugged. 'The only thing I can think of that's worse than coming with you is staying here to face Lemmon and his digger. At least this way we'll have a bit of time to think up something.'

'We'll have as much time as we like.'

It was still only seven in the morning and Trafalgar began exploring the interior of the rock while Stilts did obscure things with the screen and the keyboard.

'Hey look,' said Trafalgar, 'food.'

There was a locker full of vacuum-sealed packets marked 'self-heating pizza'. In the next cupboard was a large box of painkillers and another set of the familiar wrist-bands for remote pre-set time travel away from the time vehicle.

'What have you found?' he asked Stilts.

'Loads of stuff I don't quite understand,' Stilts mused. 'There's a full log of all the dates and coordinates for every single place we went last time, so we can easily go back again.'

Trafalgar shivered, 'That's a horrible idea.'

'There's something that says it's a howl-round pre-venter. I've switched it on for what it's worth. Don't forget we haven't finished the jobs.'

Trafalgar looked at the list. Most of them were ticked but it still said, 'JOB 15. Training wolf. Initial location: Olvisland. 3018 BC. Day 138. Midday.' It gave the usual list of coordinates, then, 'Press enter to travel.'

The thought of going back to Olvisland held few attractions but that was, after all, where they had first encountered the wolf. It had looked for a moment like being their last encounter too, because the wolf had seemed all too likely to eat them before Trafalgar, learning his way round the subtleties of time travel rather quickly, resolved the situation simply by deciding he had already been there to tame it. It had been entirely

Trafalgar 2's fault that the wolf then revealed that it had also been trained to retrieve lettuce. Trafalgar still couldn't see why he should have to be the one who put that right when it was entirely down to Trafalgar 2's carelessness in the first place.

'I suppose we have to do it,' Stilts said.

A violent twinge inside his head made up Trafalgar's mind for him. He reached for the box of painkillers, swallowed one and nodded glumly.

To kill time, he sat down at the second terminal and switched it on, intending to browse through the database, but the screen demanded a password.

'What's the password, Stilts?' he said.

'No idea. Mine didn't need one.'

Trafalgar stared at the screen, yawning. Recent events were catching up with him. After a minute or two, a screen-saver came on, starting off with a full-colour rendering of that famous pre-Sleep painting, Van Gogh's 'Hay Wain'. He smiled vaguely at it and fell deeply asleep.

Time passed. There was a loud thump on the roof and he stirred a little. There was another thump and he opened his eyes. Blinking through a dull pain in his head, he looked out through the one-way windows and saw two huge legs dangling down outside. He turned to Stilts in horror. Stilts was slumped over the keyboard, snoring. Trafalgar shook him awake, aghast.

'It's after nine,' he hissed. 'John just sat on us. Get up. We've got to get ready.'

They peered out in alarm at the digger. Lemmon was already in position at his table and they could see the time team, including their own other selves, standing around.

'That was a bad time to over-sleep,' Trafalgar whispered.

'See!' whispered Stilts. 'This is the moment when I notice the rock and I get the idea.'

Trafalgar saw the rickshaw arrive with Anya and Tito in it, and frowned at the expression on Anya's face as she waved Tito goodbye.

'OK, get ready,' Stilts murmured, 'It's nearly time.'

There were thirty seconds to go, then twenty.

'Oh sod it,' Stilts raised his hands in despair. 'We forgot to set a destination.'

'No! Er, let's er . . .'

'No time. There are only ten seconds left. What about this?'

He was back on that screen that gave them two choices, 'Last Destination' and 'Next Destination'. The cursor was on 'Next Destination.'

'What does it mean?'

'I DON'T KNOW,' said Stilts, 'I . . .'

They might have gone on arguing beyond the crucial time if a piece of the ceiling, loosened by the earlier collision, hadn't chosen that moment to drop unerringly on to the keyboard, hitting the enter key and selecting 'Next Destination.'

When things have to happen, they have to happen.

In a well-designed system, with the bugs completely ironed out of it, the screen would have displayed something mildly discouraging like 'invalid message' when the machine was asked to take itself to a destination that hadn't yet been set. Much of the electronic mechanism that made up the time machine was in essence only a very sophisticated computer. In the entire history of computers there has never been a system so well-designed that no bugs of any sort remained in it. This was no exception. The main idea of the second terminal was that the co-pilot of the time vehicle could be setting the next destination on that screen while the pilot was dealing with whatever unexpected problems time and space had joined forces to throw at him in the present location. Therefore, when the falling ceiling tile set the machine into action, it swiftly checked the second screen for instructions and found on it picture number eighty-three in the screen-saver's nearly endless array.

Nothing in the software told it to ignore a screen-saver, so it did its very best to convert the picture into a destination. It was helped in this by the fact that the picture had a caption on it.

The picture was a portrait of a woman with a faint smile on her lips and her hands crossed in front of her. In the art datafiles of 95 SEGS it was always labelled 'The Lost Supper' by Michelangelo. Many learned articles had been written analysing the wistful smile on the woman's lips. The favourite theory was that she was both absent-minded and very hungry and possibly didn't like to admit that she couldn't remember where she had left her plate. Trafalgar could sympathise with this because he often located half-eaten meals around his apartment by sitting on them, and he thought he recognised the expression on her face as someone who had just realised the cushion they were sitting on might well be a cheese omelette.

In *this* database, which Trafalgar 2 had taken great trouble to correct, knowing his less-competent predecessor needed all the help he could get as he blundered round the space-time continuum, the caption said, 'Mona Lisa. Leonardo da Vinci. Florence. 1506.' That sounded pretty much like a destination to the time machine.

There's nothing more annoying when you're trying to paint a picture than when something gets in the way of your view. Particularly when it's a cash commission for a rich customer and he wants it yesterday and you can't get his bloody wife's face to look right because she's been eating sweet things all her life and her teeth look like a row of tree-stumps after a rather severe forest fire. Leonardo had given up on the woman's mouth and was seriously wondering whether the client would object if he painted a bandanna up to nose level. Now he had turned his attention to trying to get the background sorted and he wasn't a happy man. He'd only just invented perspective and the rocks were being difficult, so he'd dragged his easel to the outskirts of town, set the picture in place on it and was just mixing up some dim browns for a particularly gnarled and twisted bush when he found he couldn't see the thing any more. There was a new rock in front of it, and a gangly youth in odd clothes was sitting on top of the rock looking about him with a wild expression on his face.

'Oy, you,' Leonardo shouted, 'get your rock out of the way. Can't you see I'm painting?'

The youth said something harsh and guttural in an alien tongue. Though it was completely incomprehensible it still managed to sound very rude indeed, and he went on sitting there. Leonardo wasn't used to that sort of thing. He put down his brush and palette and strode towards the rock, rolling up the sleeves of his smock. People thought they could push painters around, plonking their rocks down wherever they chose. He'd show them.

Then he thought he recognised the man on the rock and that made his blood boil.

Inside the rock, Trafalgar and Stilts were looking out of the window at John's legs. They didn't see the artist approaching from the side.

'He'll hop off in a minute, I bet,' said Trafalgar. 'As soon as he does, you can press the button.'

'Right,' said Stilts.

There was a shout from above them, a thump and John fell off the roof in a heap.

'Go!' shouted Trafalgar and Stilts pressed the key that took them to JOB 15.

SEVEN

The good news on landing was that the view through
the window no longer included any sign of John's legs
dangling from the top of the rock. In that respect, their
plan had worked perfectly. The bad news however, was
that another giant pair of legs was dangling in their
place. This was a considerable disappointment to both
Trafalgar and Stilts. They looked at the legs, dumb-
founded. The legs were extremely hairy, covered in
splashes of paint and ended in a pair of laced up sandals.
Of all the things they might have been expecting to see
in Olvisland in 3018 BC these were not one, or even
two.

'How did that happen?' Trafalgar cried despairingly.

'I don't know. Who is he?'

'How can I tell? All I can see is his legs.'

'Well, where was it we picked him up? And *when*,
come to that?'

'Don't you know?'

'If I did, would I be asking?'

Trafalgar stared at him in horror and spoke slowly,
'You know that plan? That clever plan you thought up
about dropping John off?'

'Yes, of course.'

'And er . . . picking him up again straight afterwards
when we'd finished.'

'That's the one.'

'Wouldn't that mean knowing where it was we
dropped him?'

'Yes. Oh, I see what you mean. Didn't you write it down?'

'No, didn't you?'

'No.'

'Let me get this straight,' said Trafalgar. 'Here we are trying hard to avoid creating any more time paradoxes, right?'

'Right.'

'Except that we've just dropped off perhaps the most unreliable and dangerous practical joker either of us have ever met somewhere in the planet's pre-Sleep history and neither of us has any idea how to get him back again?'

'Oh dear,' said Stilts, then he looked at the legs again and jerked his thumb in their direction. 'I suppose we could always ask *him*?'

Before they could take that idea any further, a furious chorus of baying arose outside. The legs jerked galvanically into life as their owner sprang from the top of the rock. They caught a brief glimpse of a flowing tunic and curly grey hair as their passenger raced away from the rock towards the shelter of the nearest tree, then he was up into the lower branches in the nick of time as a flood of huge grey shapes came pouring after him from round both sides of the rock.

They looked out at fifteen or twenty wolves, leaping, howling and generally intimating that they'd really like to get to know the man up the tree more thoroughly.

'Oh good,' said Trafalgar, 'here are the wolves. That saves us some trouble.'

'Traf?' said Stilts. 'How are you going to tell which one's Daisy?'

'I'd know her anywhere,' said Trafalgar. 'That's her!' he said, pointing as one of the wolves jumped up at the branch from which the legs of their recent passenger now dangled.

'That's a him,' said Stilts.

'Oh, so it is. No, there she is, over there. Or maybe there. Or . . .'

Wolves look quite like other wolves, even when they've been a good friend, especially when you haven't seen them for a while.

'I'll go out and see,' Trafalgar said after a long pause for thought. 'I'll soon find her, she's the only tame one.'

'Not yet, she isn't. Hang on, though, you know that thing you had in your ear?'

'The transplug?'

'Doesn't it say you can use it to talk to animals?'

Trafalgar found the box and they both studied the picture.

'That's a rabbit,' Trafalgar objected. 'We don't know if it works with wolves. Anyway, it might be some sort of joke for all we know.'

Stilts shrugged.

'Are you seriously suggesting,' said Trafalgar, 'that I should go close enough to one of those creatures out there to put one of these in its *ear*?'

'We could try it,' said Stilts, 'or we could go away and think up something else instead.'

'We can't just leave him up the tree, can we? He might be some famous historical person.'

Stilts peered up at what he could see of the scruffy paint-splashed sandals. 'He'd be better dressed if he was famous.'

'Anyway, we can't leave him. I'll try your idea with the transplug.'

'That's pretty brave,' said Stilts, impressed.

'Well, I've just remembered; I know I'm not going to die because I know it's me that does all those jobs and I haven't done them yet.'

'Good, good,' said Stilts. 'That's an excellent reason

why it should be you who goes outside, not me, now I come to think about it. I mean *my* future's still completely uncertain. I can't afford to take risks like that.'

Putting some of the transplugs in his pocket, Trafalgar opened the door cautiously and looked out at the vaguely familiar and somewhat unappealing landscape of Olvisland, full of giant versions of insects which weren't particularly attractive even when viewed on a normal scale. Off to his left, he could see the valley where one day very soon the first time team would arrive for a crash landing in the TS *Titanic*, stranding them until Stilts came up with his brilliant idea for a megalithic motherboard. Away over the hill was the village where the repulsive Olvis lived, floating above the squalor on his anti-gravity sledge. The wolves had their backs to him, concentrating on supper in the form of the man up the tree. Trafalgar took a careful step outside and the nearest wolf's nostrils twitched. He took another step and the wolf turned its head and gazed at him with an intensely curious expression. He didn't need the transplug to know what it was thinking.

It was thinking, 'I wonder what that tastes like?'

Stilts got the door closed just in time as the rock shuddered with the impact of a fast-moving, disappointed wolf and then picked Trafalgar up off the floor.

'I just had another thought,' gasped Trafalgar. 'I might simply get very badly injured and then recover horribly slowly and in constant pain.'

'Good point,' said Stilts. 'Just as well you thought of that one.'

They seemed to be stuck. The rest of the day passed slowly and the wolves, instead of going away, lay down between the rock and the tree, keeping a watchful eye on both of them. From time to time they could hear the man up the tree bellowing and they had to turn the transplug controller to maximum politeness. That way he kept saying things like, 'I really am mostly awfully irritated,' and 'Why don't you do unspeakable things to yourselves, you rather unpleasant quad-rupeds?'

Stilts had been staring into midair drumming his fingers on the control desk for several minutes when he suddenly snapped upright. 'I've got an idea,' he said and pulled open a drawer. 'Look, why don't you put on one of the remote wrist-bands. Then you can go outside and if you're about to get eaten, I can use the time machine to jump you back in here.'

'Will it work?'

'We can test it.'

'How?'

'As soon as you step out of the door, I'm going to bring you back inside just for a second to check it.'

'How do I know that will work?'

Stilts looked at the time display on the screen. 'Because I'm going to bring you back to right NOW.'

All the worst aspects of time travel immediately mani-fested themselves before their eyes – the smoke, the sudden blinding headache and in Stilts's case, the effects of having a second Trafalgar materialise in almost the same patch of floor space as the one on which he was already standing, bowling him violently over back-wards. The second Trafalgar was gone again as soon as he appeared, leaving nothing behind but two greasy footprints on the floor and a little spiral of black smoke.

'Good,' Stilts wheezed, forcing air into his lungs with some difficulty. 'It works.'

Trafalgar was trying hard not to laugh. 'Right,' he said, 'I'll do it.'

He took a painkiller and they waited for a while until

all the wolves were looking the other way, then Trafalgar slid the door open, stepped outside and closed it, bracing himself for an impact. There was a confusing second when he was inside again, crashing into Stilts, then he was back outside.

There was a significant difference.

Time travel is far from silent. It always makes a strange noise as air rushes into the instantaneous vacuum caused by the departing body, or is pushed violently outwards by the arriving body. If that wasn't enough to attract the attention of any nearby wolves, there's also the distinctive smell.

Now every single wolf was looking at him.

There was a further significant difference. He was a good distance further from the time vehicle this time. In fact he was standing on the nearest wolf's tail. It seemed only polite to get off and it seemed only sensible to run like hell. Trafalgar's mind started to work with extraordinary clarity while he was running. He wondered why Stilts hadn't immediately brought him back. He then wondered if Stilts perhaps hadn't spotted him reappearing in a different place. It then occurred to him that they should have done one more test to see if anything would go wrong by deciding that Stilts would bring him back to before he left if anything *did* go wrong. This was a complicated thought to work on while running fast and for a moment or two it stopped Trafalgar from noticing that the ground was shaking with the pounding of many feet and there was a hot, smelly wind gusting past him with subtle overtones of imperfectly cleaned teeth in it.

He glanced back and saw the entire wolf pack gaining on him rapidly.

'Stilts!' he bawled despairingly, but the pack had cut him off from the rock and every stride was taking him further away from safety. A wolf shot past him, well away to his left, and then another to his right.

'Oh fine,' he panted, 'doing the old cutting-off trick, are you?'

They were. He tried to run faster and failed. It became quite clear that unless Stilts time-lifted him out of trouble very, very soon then, time paradox or not, he was going to be eaten.

At that moment several completely unexpected things happened. First, an odd shivering sensation passed right through his body. Next, the colour of everything around him changed to shades of red. It occurred to Trafalgar that he might be having a heart attack but then he noticed that the two wolves which were out-flanking him had apparently decided it was time to take part in a shampoo commercial. They were now bouncing through the grass in exaggerated slow motion with their ears flapping gracefully. He also noticed that little puffs of smoke had started to burst from the grass wherever his feet touched it. He now ran effortlessly through the narrowing gap between the two wolves and in hardly any time at all had left them far behind. Perplexed, he ran round in a circle back towards the rock and saw the wolves, reacting very slowly to his change of direction, fall over their feet as they tried to follow and tumble slowly over in a heap. Ahead he saw the door of the rock slide very gradually open and Stilts appear as if sleepwalking, giving a 'thumbs up' sign.

Emboldened, he ran straight back through the middle of the main pack who gracefully swerved into a long-drawn-out collision of slowly tangling legs and tails. He jumped into the rock, turned and watched Stilts push the door closed. It seemed to take an age.

'What did you do?' he panted.

In a very, very deep voice, Stilts said, 'W-a-i-t,' then

moved in slow motion to the controls and touched a key. Another shiver passed through Trafalgar. Colours returned abruptly to normal and so did Stilts's voice.

'I found a new gizmo,' he said in a delighted tone. 'Fine tuning. See?'

He showed Trafalgar a very complicated screen display. 'I can change your personal time but leave you in the same place, right? I just speeded up your time so you seemed to be living much faster from my point of view. It worked a treat, didn't it?'

'Supposing it hadn't?'

'Oh, I knew it would, as soon as I saw it. Anyway, it's given me a really good idea. All you need to do is go out there and run around a lot, then they'll chase you until they're exhausted and after that it should be easy.'

'Come to that, *you* could go.'

'Well, I would of course, but I'm the one who knows how the machine works and you'll need me here to get you out of trouble if anything goes wrong.'

In fact, it turned out to be quite good fun. Trafalgar had the undivided attention of the entire, rather bruised, pack of wolves as soon as he stepped out into the open though Stilts let them get disturbingly close before he turned up the speed. Trafalgar let them chase him up and down and round and round for what seemed like hours to him until, one by one, they limped to a halt with bleeding paws and lay still, looking at him with jaundiced expressions while he walked around them. One or two tried a half-hearted snap as he got closer but it was so very easy to jump out of their way that they soon gave up even that idea and went to sleep instead.

Taking great care, Trafalgar walked up beside one likely female and pushed a transplug down into its ear.

It stirred slightly and its paws twitched but it didn't wake up. He put another plug into his own ear.

He stood back at a safe distance and said, 'Hello, wolf. How are you?'

As the first two-way conversation between a human being and another species it lacked style.

The wolf lifted its head with a startled yip and stared at him. As it growled, a voice inside Trafalgar's ear said, 'Come here so I can grind you into little juicy pieces.'

He quickly looked down at the control box but it was already on maximum politeness.

'I am your friend,' he said, trying to smile.

'Wrong. You're my lunch,' growled the wolf.

'If you do what I say, I'll give you food.'

The wolf considered. 'What sort of food?'

Trafalgar remembered the contents of the cupboard. 'Pizza?' he suggested, trying to project to the wolf a succulent image of a steaming, gooey, melting slice.

'Eugh,' said the wolf, 'where's its legs? I don't eat anything without legs. The more the better.'

'Ah, well I've only got two legs. I'm hardly worth it.'

'There's two more up there,' said the wolf thoughtfully, looking up at the tree. 'That makes four.'

Trafalgar had completely forgotten the giant in the tree. Now he looked up and saw an old, bearded man staring at the extraordinary scene below in amazement.

'I must be dreaming,' said the man in his ear.

'No, no,' said Trafalgar, 'it's all right. We'll get you down from there in a while. Just stay put.'

'What on earth is the little runt saying?' said the man and Trafalgar realised that without another transplug this was destined to be a one-way conversation. He turned his attention back to the wolf which was staring at him with disconcerting steadiness.

'One mouthful,' said the wolf, 'maybe two and you've

99

got those horrible chewy wrappings on. I wish creatures like you didn't always come with packaging, it's so bad for the environment. Still it looks easier to peel than those sheep wrappings the others wear.'

'Oh, go back to sleep,' said Trafalgar in exasperation and to his surprise the wolf did.

He retrieved the transplug from its ear with great care and tried several more wolves but none of them could see their way to a relationship with him that extended to more than treating him as a snack. He was on the verge of giving up when, wandering among the slumbering animals, he saw one she-wolf lying on her side with a little nick out of her ear and suddenly remembered the feel of that nick from stroking Daisy's head.

Excited, he pushed the transplug into the wolf's ear.

The wolf lifted her head and looked at him with polite enquiry in her eyes and started a complex series of soft whines, whimpers and little barks.

'Hello, little fast odd thing,' said the voice in Trafalgar's ear, 'that chasing game was fun.'

'Didn't you want to catch me?'

'Not really. I'm thinking of becoming a vegetarian.'

'Can wolves do that?'

'Am I a wolf?'

'That's what we call you. What do you call you?'

'We call us "us".'

'I'm Trafalgar.'

'I'm me.'

'Can I call you "Daisy"?'

'You probably can. It doesn't sound hard. Try it and see.'

'No, I mean would you like your name to be Daisy?'

'A name of my own? Just for me? Yes, please.'

'I could teach you quite a lot of other things if you like.'

100

'That sounds like fun.'

Trafalgar looked around at all the other slumbering wolves.

'Um, is there any way of getting rid of the rest of your friends?'

'Friends? Friends! They're the pack. They're no friends of mine. I always wanted to be a lone wolf. You want me to get rid of them?'

'Yes please.'

'Watch this.' She got to her feet then seemed to think twice about it. 'You'd better hide somewhere,' she said. 'They may get a bit overexcited.'

Trafalgar ran over to the rock and got behind it. The wolf began to caper in circles, leaping into the air and howling every few steps. As amateur acting goes, it was quite a performance.

'Wake up, wake up,' she yelled. 'A huge herd of animals just went by.'

'Shut it,' said a big wolf, crossly. 'I'm tired.' Then he started to dribble. 'What sort of animals?' he said.

'The nice, meaty sort with thin legs.'

He got to his feet and a few more wolves followed him. He stood there uncertainly.

'The question is,' he said, 'can I be bothered?'

'There's men coming from the other way,' Daisy improvised wildly. 'Men with sticks.'

'How do you know?' said the big wolf, rudely.

'A bird told me.'

One or two wolves lifted their heads and sniffed the air.

'The sticks have got points on.'

'Birds never tell *me* things,' said the big wolf. 'What you doing talking to bleeding birds anyway?'

The rest of the wolves got nervously to their feet.

'The men are coming from upwind . . . and they've got fire, too.'

That did it. There was a chorus of nervous yelps and entire pack took off at high speed in a downwind direction. Daisy sat there looking rather pleased.

Stilts opened the door of the rock and came out with a relieved expression. At that point there was a barrage of words from above their heads and they remembered the man in the tree. Stilts could only hear an incomprehensible babble. Trafalgar, with the transplug in his ear, could unfortunately understand every word of the tirade.

'I want to get down and I want to get down NOW,' the man was shouting. 'I am a very important man and I shall be complaining about this to the authorities. I am on very good terms with the Borgias, and particularly Pope Alexander and the Duke of Milan. I have to finish a VERY IMPORTANT PICTURE by next week. You're far too small to kidnap me. Wolves are dangerous animals and they should be kept under control. It's ridiculous and anyway I'm very hungry.'

Daisy could also understand him.

'Why doesn't the noisy one climb down?' she asked.

'I expect he thinks you might eat him,' said Trafalgar.

'No, really?' Daisy sounded genuinely shocked. She walked over to the base of the tree, wagged her tail, rolled over on her back and waved her paws in the air enticingly.

'What's it DOING?' the man howled.

'I'll have to go up and talk to him,' said Trafalgar crossly. 'Daisy, just don't do anything that looks threatening.' She sat up and begged.

'Oh no, that's HORRIBLE,' roared the man in the tree.

'Maybe you'd better just lie down and keep still.' Trafalgar patted her on the head then began to climb the trunk.

'GO AWAY. You're not real. I don't believe in you. Come any nearer and I'll swat you off the branch.'

It took a while to persuade him by sign language that he should put the plug in his ear.

'Sir,' said Trafalgar politely. 'This wolf is quite safe. It's a friend of mine. You can come down.'

'Who are you? Why are you so small? Where am I? How did I get here? How can I get home?'

'I'm Trafalgar,' he said as that seemed to be the only one of the questions which had anything like an acceptable answer. 'Can we leave the rest of it until later?'

'I WANT TO GO HOME!'

'He wants to go home,' Trafalgar said to Stilts.

'Ask him where home is.'

'Where is your home?'

The man stared wildly around. 'Florence, of course. What have you done with it? Where has it gone? Have you hidden it?'

'Ask him when,' called Stilts from below.

'Right,' said Trafalgar and looked apprehensively at the old man. 'Er, do you happen to know what date it is today?'

The old man's arm moved violently.

Falling off the tree didn't hurt a bit. It was landing that did, though it may have hurt Daisy more because Trafalgar landed on her. He picked himself up, turned the knob on the control unit down to minimum politeness and let off a few choice swearwords. The box grew warm to the touch as it selected suitable sixteenth-century Italian equivalents and the man up the tree grew even warmer as he replied in kind.

'May your guts putrefy within you, you excrement-coated son of a . . .'

Daisy growled and Trafalgar turned the knob as far as it would go the other way '. . . not entirely pleasant

103

woman whose personal habits left a teensy bit to be desired. May your next-door neighbour suffer occasionally from almost unnoticeable aches and I hope your socks never match . . .'

It was getting dark rapidly and the man clearly had no intention whatsoever of coming down from the tree. Trafalgar felt extraordinarily weary, but then he had been travelling for the last five thousand, seven hundred and twenty five years.

'Let's get some sleep,' he said. 'Maybe he'll be more friendly in the morning.' That provoked another burst of shouting from the tree. Trafalgar looked at Daisy. 'See he doesn't come to any harm, will you?' She wagged her tail.

EIGHT

Trafalgar and Stilts were glad to have the rock that night. The sofa folded out to form a comfortable bed and the closed door protected them against any outsize horrors that might have been wandering around in the dark. Trafalgar wasn't worried about Daisy, knowing that not only was she quite capable of looking after herself but also that past history showed her immediate future was quite safe. He was much more concerned about the safety of the old man up the tree. If something had happened to him then Trafalgar was pretty sure that the time paradox involved in allowing a citizen of the sixteenth century to be killed thousands of years before he was born would prove to be a real headache. He slept uneasily and the first thing he did on waking up was to look out through the window. For a moment he was horrified to see that there was nobody in the tree. On the ground, however, there was an unexpected sight. The old man had come down and was sitting next to the wolf talking animatedly and scratching diagrams in the earth with a stick. The wolf, judging from the noises it was making, seemed to be taking part in an earnest discussion.

'What's going on?' said Stilts.

'I haven't a clue,' Trafalgar replied. 'Let's go and see.' He opened the door and they went out.

'Good morning,' Trafalgar said. Daisy lifted her head, wagged her tail and slobbered at him cheerfully. The old man looked annoyed at the interruption and held up his hand for silence. He went on drawing with his stick and they went closer to see what was going on. The patch of earth around his feet was a maze of overlapping lines.

Nothing could interrupt the flow of the old man's lecture.

'. . . and then to get the proportions right,' he was saying, 'you must make sure that the dimensions of the lintel across the top of the columns is in complete harmony with the diameter of the columns. Now, when you use *Doric* columns to get that classical look to your facade, you should really . . .'

'Excuse me,' said Trafalgar with the knob turned to give just a little extra politeness for safety's sake. 'What exactly are you doing?'

'Do you have to interrupt?' said the man. 'I'm busy teaching the rudiments of art. We've gone right through painting and sculpture. Now we're on architecture. Isn't it obvious?'

'Why? She's a wolf.'

'So? She *listens*. She understands what I say. I have never had such a willing student. What does it matter if she's a wolf? Have you got something against wolves? Eh? She asks intelligent questions. If she has nothing to say she keeps quiet and best of all she doesn't *fidget*.'

'She's a supine lupine, you mean?'

Weak puns relying on rhyme were well beyond the scope of the transplug.

'That's what I just said,' the man responded crossly. 'You've spoilt it now. I'll have to go back over the whole of the columns section.'

'Ah, well. Hold on just a minute. The fact is I need her for a bit. There's something I've got to teach her too. That's why we're here.'

'You? You teach her?' He laughed rudely. 'I, Leonardo, I am the most noted artist of this age. Young

Michelangelo Buonarroti is a mere decorator by comparison. People come from all over Italy to study at my feet. What can you teach her that could matter more than the golden secrets of my own skills?'

'I've got to . . .' Trafalgar was about to say, 'I've got to teach her to identify and fetch on command a particular species of primitive wild lettuce,' but it didn't seem quite the right thing under the circumstances.

'. . . do something very important,' he ended lamely. He considered not bothering about the lettuce which was, after all, the product of an ill-judged series of comments by Trafalgar 2 and therefore not really his fault, but he was immediately hit by such a hot stab of headache that he gave up the idea immediately.

He addressed himself to the wolf, 'Daisy. I need you.'

The wolf looked back at him affably. 'Eh?' it said.

'I need you for some important training.'

'Eh?'

'You can come back and learn about architecture afterwards.'

'Eh?'

'I think her plug must have fallen out,' said Stilts helpfully. 'Yes, look. There it is on the ground.'

'Oh yes.' He picked it up and pushed it back into the wolf's ear.

Leonardo threw up his hands in despair. 'No, no. How much has she missed? I'll have to start again.'

Daisy yipped, 'I got it all up to the bit on friezes and architraves.'

'Now, sorry, Daisy,' said Trafalgar, 'but I need your full attention for a few minutes.'

The wolf grinned at him.

'I want you to fetch me a lettuce.'

She jumped up, looking excited, and fetched him the stick which Leonardo had been using.

'No, that's a stick. Do you know what a lettuce is?'

Her answer, broadly speaking, was that she had no idea at all but was very happy to go on fetching things until she hit on the right one. In the course of the next few minutes he taught her lots of useful things, such as 'Sit,' 'Lie down,' and 'Roll over,' and she brought him as many different objects as she could find in the immediate vicinity. This didn't go far beyond sticks, rocks, lumps of earth and something dry and furry which had been dead for quite a long time.

Leonardo, who was listening intently to all of this with an annoyed expression, kept looking at Trafalgar as if he were mad.

'Why do you ask her to do these foolish things?' he said scornfully. 'She is no fetcher of lettuces. She is potentially the greatest student of the arts in the entire kingdom of animals. She could achieve more in the field of architecture than any wolf before her.'

'That might not be too hard,' muttered Stilts.

'Look, it's very simple,' said Trafalgar. 'Last time I met her, Trafalgar 2, that's to say me, but a later version of me, told me not to tell her to go and fetch a lettuce because if she did, that meant one of us would already have had to come back to train her to do it, but accidentally, by telling me *not* to, he said the word "lettuce" in her hearing and she went off and fetched one, so now I have to do it. The training, I mean.'

'Very simple?' said Leonardo with a glazed expression. 'That is very simple? Well anyway, you are not an artist, obviously. You do not have the power to discern, to imagine, to describe.'

'Fine. Look, I'll do you a deal,' said Trafalgar. 'It's got to be done. You talk to her. Explain about lettuce. Get it over with then you can go on with the art lessons.'

It was now several thousand years since Leonardo had last eaten. Thinking of lettuce brought that painfully to mind. 'I'm hungry,' he said.

'I'll make you some food if you'll just tell her about lettuce.'

Leonardo considered the alternatives. Hunger won.

'All right,' he said sulkily, 'I'll tell her.'

Trafalgar went to cook the self-heating pizzas which only required pulling the tag on the packets. Weighing one in his hand, he decided Leonardo would probably need at least twenty. They were the usual unsatisfactory fast-food pizza, unappetising discs of semi-industrial dough, topped with a thick layer of what were probably supposed to be deep-fried processed strawberries in an unrealistic shade of purple. The top surface was covered in the sort of not-exactly-cheese that seems to get bigger and bigger in your mouth as you chew it.

Leonardo ate the first one and an odd expression passed over his face. He ate another rather more slowly,

'A good idea, badly executed,' he said. 'It will never catch on like this.' He tried another. 'Better dough, mozzarella, a little olive oil and some tomatoes and maybe it has possibilities. Cooked perhaps in a wood-fired oven, flavoured by just a sprinkle of oregano? It could have promise.'

'Have you told Daisy what we want?'

'Yes,' he said through his mouthful. 'I have even drawn her a picture of a lettuce. She says she has never seen a plant anything like it around here.'

This was not surprising as the crisp frizzy Italian lettuce he had described was the product of careful and selective market gardening and would not make its appearance in the gastronomic world for several more millennia. The lettuce of Olvis's time looked, and was, almost completely unappetising, being mostly sought after by delegations of slugs in need of a handy conference centre. Not knowing this, however, Daisy dutifully spent the next few hours fruitlessly searching the countryside for two or three miles around.

It was Stilts who came up with a quick answer.

'Daisy doesn't know where to find it, does she?'

'No. It could take ages and if it does we're going to run out of pizza at the rate *he's* eating them.'

'But she does know where they are later on, doesn't she? Because she's going to bring you some when we come back the first time?'

Trafalgar thought back to their previous visit to Olvisland. 'Yes. She made O'Barron eat a whole one.'

'Simple, then. Let's go and get Daisy from the future and bring her back here so she can tell this Daisy where to find it.'

'Sounds good. Oh, no it doesn't.'

'Why not?'

'Where do you suggest we go to get her?'

'Anywhere where no one will notice.'

'She was never out of my sight, not once.'

'Literally never?'

'No. Not from when she first fetched the lettuce right through to when she finally floated away on the anti-gravity sledge.'

Stilts knew perfectly well that trying to change things which had already happened was always doomed to end in failure.

'All right,' he said, 'let's go and get her *after* she floated off.'

The idea was appealing. It had almost broken Trafalgar's heart to see Daisy sailing off into the sky, borne away on the wind on the anti-gravity sledge. He hated not knowing what was going to happen to her.

'But we don't know where she went.'

110

'We could try looking in the datastores,' suggested Stilts.

'What? Under "Daisy"? Hardly.'

'She's a very unusual wolf. We could search for stories about friendly wolves that help people. There might be something.'

There was.

They could have just asked Leonardo but they had no idea that he was an expert on ancient Rome.

In the version of history that was current in 95 SEGS, much altered by the attentions of the descendants of John's mice, the datastore entry for Romulus read 'German General of Second World War, known as Desert Fox because of his habit of quietly stealing other people's puddings'. For Remus, it simply said 'Anagram of serum, sumer, rumes, muser and esrum.' These were not helpful but fortunately no one in the post-Sleep world had ever bothered to look at either entry, knowledge not being high up their scale of priorities, so that didn't matter.

Fortunately the datastore now in the time machine had been corrected and didn't contain any of this nonsense. What it said was: 'Romulus and Remus: Legendary founders of the city of Rome in the year 753 BC. Twin sons of the Vestal Virgin, Rhea Silvia. In a power struggle over who should run the kingdom, the babies were thrown into the River Tiber in a basket. A she-wolf, coming to the river to drink, was attracted by their cries, rescued them, licked them clean and kept them alive with her milk until the shepherd Faustulus took them to his wife Larentia to be brought up.'

'Hey, look at that! That sounds like the sort of thing Daisy would do,' said Trafalgar, excited.

'It says it's a legend,' Stilts pointed out.

'There's no harm in trying.'

That hadn't been their experience so far. There had turned out to be harm in almost every single thing they had tried since they first began time travelling, but neither of them could come up with anything better.

'Shall we take those two with us?'

'No,' said Stilts. 'We'll come straight back. They won't even know we've gone.'

They took careful note of their precise time and space coordinates and recorded it in the machine. Then Stilts typed in all that they knew of their destination. 'Rome. 753 BC. Banks of River Tiber next to two babies in a basket.'

'Taken your pill?' Stilts asked.

'Yes.'

'Get ready then.'

The time jump was worse than usual. Trafalgar felt as if a giant drain cleaner was attacking both his ears with rubber plungers. It went on and on as the time machine hunted for its target throughout pre-Christian Rome. The nearest babies it could find in a basket were in 812 BC and even then it was hardly a basket, being more of a wooden trug, but the machine had been built with a high compromise factor so it rightly accepted that as the best fit.

They arrived in a damp, boggy place – a marshy river valley in a plain broken up by seven low hills. The rock came to rest on a spit of firm land on the outside of a bend in the river but when they climbed out, they only took two steps before plunging up to their knees in mud. Ahead of them, a low island divided the river and away to their right at the top of the nearest hill, smoke rose from cooking fires in a circle of rough huts. It aroused unwelcome memories of Olvis's village and neither of them had the slightest wish to go closer.

'Stand still,' said Stilts. 'I think I can hear something.'

A faint cry, like a distant bird, came to their ears.

'Over there,' said Trafalgar, pointing.

They waded through huge reeds in the direction of the sound, which grew gradually louder and louder. By the time they got to the middle of the thickest clump the cries had become deafening, and there they found a trug the size of a small boat. Inside it, wrapped up in dirty rags, were two six-foot babies who were clearly very hungry indeed.

'Right,' said Trafalgar, 'all we need now is Daisy.'

'Ah,' said Stilts. 'Now I meant to ask you about that bit. What makes you think she's going to come here?'

They turned to the maps in the datastores – maps with strange, alien names on them like 'America' and 'France'. These would have been quite startling to any other travellers from the post-Sleep period but Trafalgar and Stilts had been through that. They knew that countries had different names then.

'It's in the right direction,' Trafalgar said. 'Last time we saw Daisy the wind was taking her off to the south-east. It ties in with the legend. She must be coming here and if these are the two she rescues, she's bound to turn up soon. I reckon we've just got to wait a bit and she'll show up.'

'She can't. You haven't thought about dates, have you? What year is it?'

'812 BC.'

'What year was it when we saw Daisy leave Olvisland?'

'3018 BC. . . Oh dear, I see what you mean. We're in for a long wait.'

'No we're not,' said Stilts, exasperated. 'You still haven't got the hang of these dates, have you? It's the other way round. Listen, the year zero SEGs is the same as the year 2612 AD which must stand for after

113

something or other. Then you get back to zero AD and you start counting backwards into BC which probably stands for "backward counting." Is that clear.'

'Yes . . . Well, no.'

'Just take it from me. It means Daisy would have got here two thousand, two hundred and six years ago.'

'So . . . she's not likely to be around still?'

'Correct.'

'And these babies aren't going to get fed?'

'Not unless there happens to be another nice wolf lurking around.'

Trafalgar stared around at what he could see through the reeds of the immediate area. It didn't seem likely. 'We could go and get her and bring her here,' he suggested. 'It couldn't do any harm, could it? They're sweet babies and they sound *so* hungry.'

Stilts imagined trying to change a nappy on a baby slightly larger than himself and decided some outside help might be a very good idea.

Back in the rock an obvious difficulty cropped up.

'Right,' said Stilts, settling down at the controls, 'where do we find Daisy?'

'Er . . .'

This seemed to be an insoluble problem. When they'd last seen Daisy, she had been several hundred feet up in the air, blowing gently along on Olvis's anti-gravity sledge. Even if they could work out likely coordinates, the rock didn't seem capable of staying up there in mid-air all by itself, let alone the collision risk. It seemed much more likely it would drop like a stone, or even like a rock.

'Right,' said Stilts. 'We'll have to do it the hard way. The log of the last journey gives us the time/space coordinates of where we were when she left and we know she was going roughly south-east. So let's say we

114

go back there, but somewhere ten miles down her flight path so we'll see her go over.'

'Then what?'

'We'll just have to go on doing that, one jump at a time, until she comes down to earth.'

'Wait! We can save ourselves all that trouble. All we have to do is come back here, say in a minute's time when we've found *where that is*, and tell us *now* and we can go straight . . . ugh.'

'Headache?' said Stilts with sympathy. 'Don't even start to think thoughts like that.'

'Why don't we just try right here? We could go back to the right date and have a quick look.'

'What possible reason could we have for doing that? That's absurd. Come on, we'll just have to do it the hard way.'

Their first landing was right in the middle of the village of the next tribe but two from Olvis's people. The rock caused a certain amount of structural damage, though the village was so badly built that it was hard to tell. In the ensuing chaos, Trafalgar had time to nip outside, look quickly up at the speck in the sky and register the fact that the changing wind was now taking it off to the west.

It would be possible in the centuries after that date to plot the route Daisy took in the course of the next two days by the prevalence of local legends about tiny people who could suddenly appear and disappear. Back in Olvisland, Cliff the shepherdess was already taking to her new role of storyteller with zeal, spreading the tales of the elves, as she would insist on calling the ELV time team. The wind now blew Daisy all the way across to the southern part of Ireland where it only took three sightings of Trafalgar and Stilts by the big people to get the leprechaun tradition going full-swing.

One hundred and eighteen stops later, an exhausted and aching Trafalgar finally saw the anti-gravity sledge come gently to rest at more or less exactly the spot next to the River Tiber where they had started from.

'Absurd, eh?' he said to Stilts.

'Ho bloody ho,' said Stilts, stiffly. He didn't seem to want to prolong the conversation.

Daisy was extremely pleased to see them and very hungry indeed after her trip so they gave her half the remaining stock of pizzas and slipped in a painkiller for the trip ahead. Trafalgar used the transplug to explain what they wanted her to do about the lettuce and, leaving the anti-gravity sledge concealed in the reeds, he asked her to jump up on the roof of the rock for the hop back to Olvisland.

Leonardo had not entirely understood anything that had happened to him since the rock had first arrived in his life. It seemed easier on balance to go along with it all than to try to wrestle the facts into shape. He found the wolf somehow less disturbing than the two very small people and he'd taken comfort in talking through the details of his art with the animal. It helped him ignore everything else that was happening to him.

It was hard to ignore the *second* wolf. He had been looking at the rock, vaguely wishing it would go away when it did. It was only gone for a moment but when it came back again, there was the second wolf sitting calmly on top of it and Daisy, sitting next to him studying his diagram on the rule of the golden third which governs aesthetics, looked up in surprise and whimpered.

The second wolf jumped off the rock, crossed over to them and let out a series of rather bossy-sounding yips. It had an extraordinary effect on Daisy who looked as astonished as it is possible for a wolf to look, then lay down with her front paws over her eyes, lifting them one at a time for an occasional peek. This was a normal reaction for a wolf who has just been told that another wolf is in fact a second version of herself and who is suffering, for the first time in her life, from a violent headache. It also had an extraordinary effect on Leonardo who, with the benefit of the transplug, was able to eavesdrop on the whole conversation. Wolves have a limited vocabulary when it comes to abstract concepts so it took a long time for Daisy 2 to explain. When she had done, both wolves got up and trotted off to the far-off lettuce patch, leaving the Italian painter scratching his head.

NINE

It took a while to find the right way to persuade Leonardo to sit on the rock. Trafalgar and Stilts couldn't wait to shake the dust of 3018 BC off their feet. It was not their favourite place but it was not a simple matter of jumping in the rock and racing off. Leonardo was in a difficult mood.

'Why should I?' he said.

'Surely you don't want to stay here?'

'Why not?'

'Because it's not a very nice place.'

Leonardo looked round and sniffed. 'I think it is.'

'You haven't met Olvis,' said Stilts under his breath.

'You can't stay here,' said Trafalgar desperately. 'You'll never get home if you stay here.'

'I don't see why not,' said Leonardo looking around the horizon. 'I'll admit I don't actually recognise the immediate vicinity but we can't have gone far in the landslide.'

'Landslide?' said Trafalgar aghast.

'Well, I assume it was a landslide. How else could the rock have rolled here?'

'I don't think you've quite got the hang of this yet,' Stilts said cautiously. 'You see what actually happened is . . .'

Trafalgar broke in quickly, feeling an explanation wasn't really likely to help.

'We'll explain later,' he said. 'Actually you'd be surprised how far we've come. I don't think you'll get back by yourself. Just try sitting on top and there'll be another landslide along shortly.'

'No,' said Leonardo.

As if that wasn't enough they had a choice of wolves. Daisy 1 and Daisy 2 had come back together with the training complete, each proudly carrying a stringy specimen of early lettuce and putting immense pressure on Trafalgar and Stilts by means of hurt looks to eat the horrid stuff. Luckily they soon found they could drop it leaf by leaf into the surrounding undergrowth and the wolves were none the wiser. Clearly one wolf had to stay in Olvisland ready to meet the imminent arrival of the *Titanic* and the other needed to come with the rock but as they looked absolutely identical it wasn't immediately clear which one to pick.

'Does it matter?' Stilts wondered aloud.

'Of course it does,' said Trafalgar indignantly. 'Think it through. If we take the wrong wolf to Rome on the rock, the other one will be stuck in a loop. It's a dreadful thought, just imagine it. The poor thing would keep getting as far as Rome on the sledge, then being brought back here. It would go on and on like that.'

That at least solved the first problem because Leonardo, plug firmly in his ear, was eavesdropping. Hearing that they were heading for Rome seemed to change his attitude entirely. He couldn't wait to get on top of the rock.

'Rome!' he said. 'Bellissima Roma! City of Cities. When a man is tired of Rome, he is tired of life!' (This was the first of many variations on a theme, which by the time it got to 95 SEGS, had become 'When a man is tired of life, he's ready for bed.')

'And from Rome,' he went on, 'I know my way back to Florence so all will be well. Come on now, where's this landslide?'

'He's going to find it hard to get the hang of this time

travel business, isn't he?' said Stilts, forgetting for a moment that Leonardo could overhear him.

'What is this time travel?' said the artist.

'It's definitely time to travel. Yup, definitely,' said Stilts hastily but Leonardo gave him a questioning look and sat there, staring into space with a thoughtful expression on his face.

They had to cross-examine the two wolves to find out which one was which. This took some time. In the end, it was clear that one of them knew all about the time team, Olvis and airborne sledge rides and the other, though guessing happily and thoroughly enjoying the new game, didn't have a clue about any of these things. When they were finally satisfied, they told Daisy 2 to jump up on top of the rock as well. Leonardo took the opportunity to launch into a fresh lecture.

'You must never rely merely on colour for your contrast. Atmosphere is best created by chiaroscuro, the use of light and shadow in a narrow array of similar shades . . .'

The wolf, who didn't have a transplug in her ear, gave him an indulgent smile and nodded occasionally to keep him happy.

There seemed no point in trying to explain to Daisy 1 that she'd soon be meeting them the first time round or telling her where to go because they knew it was going to happen anyway. They waved goodbye to her as she sat there looking dejected and abandoned in advance, being good at moral blackmail, then they set course for the River Tiber again.

Thus it was that help arrived for the starving twins in the form of the rock, loaded with Trafalgar and Stilts plus the future world's most famous artist and the wolf, although only the last of these ever gets any credit in the stories. Fortified by the headache pills, they passed through the momentary nausea of the journey, landing with a lurch and a sound of splintering to find they had come down a short distance from where they had landed before. The rock now sat on the ground in the middle of what seemed to be a pile of firewood. Trafalgar and Stilts clambered out and attempted to lead the other two back through the marshes but Daisy sniffed the air, listened for a moment and bounded ahead whining, with Leonardo following so fast that the smaller pair with their much shorter legs couldn't keep up. Daisy seemed to need no instructions and clearly had a very strong maternal instinct. When she reached the babies, she gave their faces a good licking and tried to drag the trug to dry land but Leonardo picked it up for her and carried it back to the rock, passing Trafalgar and Stilts who were still only halfway there, laboriously trudging through the mud. They swore and turned round. By the time they got back, considerably out of breath, the others were sitting by the rock and Daisy was finishing the job of cleaning up the twins.

Leonardo was looking extremely disappointed and he swung round to attack Trafalgar. 'You said we were going to Rome,' he said bitterly. 'This is not Rome. This land-slide thing, maybe it doesn't work so well, eh? I don't know this place. Where is Rome? I want to go to Rome. I demand to go to Rome. Why do we stop for these babies?'

Trafalgar looked round at the empty landscape. 'Patience,' he said. 'It'll be along one day. First things first, these two need feeding.'

'Give them some of that pizza stuff,' said Leonardo, grumpily. 'What do you mean, it'll be along?'

Trafalgar was more concerned with the children. 'Pizza's no good. I think it has to be wolf milk. That's what the story said.'

'Ha! No baby is going to drink wolf milk,' said

Leonardo dismissively. 'Not unless they are Romulus and Remus.' He laughed derisively.

'Which one is which, do you think?' said Trafalgar. 'Well, I suppose it's up to us really. Let's say that one's Romulus, the one with the dimple.'

In the long, long silence which followed, Leonardo peered closely at the twins in disbelief as they took enthusiastically to being fed by Daisy. Next he stared long and hard at the course of the river, the island in the middle and then at the seven hills.

'I know ancient Rome well, you know,' he remarked conversationally, 'I've studied its history, its culture, its religion and its architecture. Otherwise I wouldn't believe any of this because it's *bonkers*, it's . . .' his voice rose in pitch, '. . . it's *barmy*. It makes *no sense at all*.' He pointed to one of the hills. 'But I know, you see? I know the geography. I know it cannot possibly be and yet I recognise that hill. And that one, and that one.' He gave a little sob, 'Shall I prove it? Eh? Eh? This one here, the nearest, this is the Palatine Hill. That one is the Capitoline. There's the Verminal and the Quirinal. That one over there is the . . .'

'OK, I believe you,' said Trafalgar quickly.

'They'll build all over them one day, you know. Wonderful buildings. An inspiration to my own age, rivalling the very best that our own architects can design. Palaces, piazzas, temples. Oh how I wish I had designed those buildings. Would you like to know where they'll put them all? Look, just here there'll be the Forum and . . .'

'No, no. That's fine really. Oh hang on a minute, there's somebody coming,' Trafalgar said in relief.

Faustulus was not a complicated man. He was a simple herdsman. When he saw a wolf feeding two babies, he thought, 'Oh look, there's a wolf feeding two babies.' The next thing he thought was 'What's that rock doing where our temple ought to be?'

He looked at the splintered wood sticking out from under the rock and addressed himself sternly to the old bloke (What have you done to our temple?).

'I'm fluent in Latin,' Leonardo said quickly to Trafalgar. 'I can handle this.' He took the plug out of his ear. 'GREETINGS FRIEND. I AM LEONARDO. THESE SMALL PEOPLE ARE MY COMPANIONS. DO NOT FEAR THE WOLF, IT IS A FRIEND.'

(Stop talking gibberish, you old goat and tell me what you've done with our temple,) Faustulus spluttered.

'I don't think he understood you,' said Trafalgar.

'What a coarse and primitive man. If that is Latin then it's the worst Latin I ever heard. Horrible. Sounds more like a dialect of Etruscan to me.'

(Stop talking to the kid and tell me how this rock got here,) said Faustulus, his face turning red.

Trafalgar reached into his pocket and held out a trans-plug to the new arrival. Faustulus reached out and took it. He looked at it suspiciously, sniffed it and licked it. Trafalgar mimed putting it in his ear. Faustulus suddenly beamed, an expression of understanding dawning on his face. He nodded and, reaching out, tried to shove it in Trafalgar's ear. As there was already a plug in that ear this proved difficult, so Faustulus pushed harder and harder.

'Stop it,' said Trafalgar, trying to get away, and the wolf, still suckling the two hungry babies, growled disapprovingly. Stilts crept surreptitiously into the rock.

Trafalgar carefully repeated the mime with the plug then pointed at Faustulus who immediately turned round to look behind him to see what Trafalgar was pointing at. Giving up, Trafalgar went up to the giant

123

man to try to insert the plug himself but, stretching as high as he could, he could only reach a little above the man's knees. Just then there was a blurred flash as an insubstantial shape shot out of the rock's door leaving a trail of smouldering grass along the ground and seemed to swarm with enormous speed up the herdsman's smock which was pulled and tugged violently.

Faustulus's head was jerked slightly to one side and then the shape shot off back to the rock. Scorched patches smouldered acridly all up one side of the man's clothing.

'What the bloody hell was that?' said the herdsman's translated voice in Trafalgar's ear.

'Well done, Stilts,' said Trafalgar. 'Good thinking.'

'Don't mention it,' said Stilts coming back out of the rock at a normal pace. 'I had the speed turned right up.'

'Let's try again, then,' said Trafalgar politely. 'What were you saying, sir?'

'I was talking to your dad. I asked him what he'd done to the temple.' He pointed at the splintered wood under the rock. 'It's all broken. You dropped your rock on it.'

Whose temple was it?' asked Leonardo.

'It was Mars.'

'Mars?' said Leonardo and turned to whisper to Trafalgar. 'I knew it. It passes all understanding but we *are* in the right place. Mars was the Roman God of War, you know.'

'Yes, Mars,' said Faustulus, 'and she's going to be very, very cross.'

'She?' Leonardo turned and whispered again. 'Ignorant savage. Mars is a he, not a she.'

'I heard that,' said Faustulus indignantly. 'You think I don't know my shes from my hes? You'd be a brave man to tell *her* that. Probably hurl something at you, she would.'

'A thunderbolt perhaps?'

'No, don't be daft. More likely that big stick she's carrying. Here she comes now.'

They turned and gaped at a huge person who was striding down from the hill behind them, staring grimly at the wreckage under the rock. It was waving a stick made from a small tree trunk and it wasn't a woman in any normal sense of the word. It looked more like an approaching accident of a very violent nature.

'Who's that?' gasped Leonardo.

'Who do you think it is? Like I've been trying to tell you, that's Ma and she's coming to ask what you've done to her temple.'

A brief note on the nature of transplugs might help. They were designed in the far-off future long after 95 SEGS purely for recreational reasons in a time when everyone except the occasional visiting alien spoke the same language. As the packaging had suggested they were really meant to allow people to converse with household pets who didn't have a particularly wide or varied vocabulary and it had never really been intended that they would be used for anything more challenging. Certainly the way Trafalgar and Stilts were now using them was well outside the manufacturers' original intentions and they would have denied all liability for subsequent events.

The basic principle was simple. Words are triggered first of all by thoughts, excluding perhaps those uttered by politicians, drunks or some song writers. These thoughts are shaped by the brain into words but the transplug simply picked up the thoughts in their purest form before the point where they passed from the brain through the neural connections on their way to the vocal cords and were turned into language. It then transmitted them to other nearby transplugs where they were fed back into the pathway from the ear to the brain as pure thought. This cut out the need for clumsy translation completely.

It did however cause a few problems when it came to vague, abstract concepts beyond the usual scope of household pets; concepts concerning, let's say, spiritual or religious matters. The word 'temple' is a case in point. Religion didn't really figure in the post-Sleep world due to the mess the mice had made of the datastores but Trafalgar and Stilts had come across the idea of a temple on their previous trip when they'd helped create what later became Stonehenge out of an incomplete flatpack temple with misleading assembly instructions foisted on Olvis by some fly-by-night salesman. Leonardo, of course, had a perfectly clear idea of what a temple was. In this case, however, 'temple' was simply the nearest the transplug had been able to get to what Faustulus meant. What Faustulus meant was an important place where some members of his tribe could go when they needed a period of peace for the completion of a ritual which had a special significance for them involving deep thought, concentration and ceremonial cleansing.

'Lavatory' would have been a much better word.

(All right then. Whose rock's this then?) said Faustulus's Ma when all the different bits of her came to a halt.

'It's their rock, Ma. It wasn't anything to do with me, honest,' said Faustulus.

Trafalgar stared at her, fascinated. The helmet went well with her beard and the bearskin she was wearing smelt as though it still had quite a bit of bear attached to the inside. She made him feel about a foot tall, which was exactly what he was, of course. This was a good thing as she was fairly short-sighted and completely failed to notice him and Stilts.

Leonardo decided to try charm, though she didn't look like the sort of person on whom it would make much impact. Come to that, she didn't look like the sort of person on whom a well-wielded battle-axe would make much impact either.

'Dear lady, please let me apologise. We had no intention at all of . . .'

(What's he jabbering about? Don't he know how to speak proper Etruscan Sabine hybrid lower Tiber Valley dialect?)

'Do your trick again, Stilts,' whispered Trafalgar.

'You do it,' he hissed back. 'I don't fancy climbing *that* one bit.'

There was no time to argue. They slipped into the rock and Trafalgar put on the wrist-band.

'Maximum speed,' said Stilts. 'Take the plug out of your pocket first.'

'Why?'

'You might set your clothes on fire reaching for it. Are you ready? Here goes.'

The world turned deep red and everything came to an almost complete halt. A drop of sweat, falling from Leonardo's nose, moved almost imperceptibly towards the ground. Trafalgar walked to the giant woman's feet, took a firm hold on the bottom of the bearskin and climbed up it. It took nerve and a certain amount of technical skill to get round the overhangs but he'd done some mountain climbing as a student and the techniques stood him in good stead. The bearskin was alive with various large insects but they were behaving as if nearly paralysed so he used them as extra handholds.

He reached her shoulder, grabbed her ear lobe for support as she slowly began to react to his weight, and plunged the plug in through the forest of hair which bristled out of the hole. Then, noticing how light he seemed in time-adjusted gravity, he jumped off, floated down to the ground and scorched back into the rock.

Time returned to normal and now everyone there could talk to everyone else except Daisy and the babies who seemed to be in a cosy, private world of their own.

'Dear lady,' said Leonardo again, 'we will rebuild your temple for you magnificently. It will be the finest temple ever seen.'

She snorted. 'I liked it just the way it was. You'll have to do better than that.'

'Turn up the politeness,' Stilts urged quietly.

Trafalgar turned the knob.

'It will be far better than you deserve, you miserable old bag,' said Leonardo. 'I'm offering to put up an architectural wonder instead of that undoubtedly hideous and ramshackle hut you had before. Frankly your facial hair and your attitude make me want to vomit equally. We'll build it for you if we have to but if falls on your foul-smelling head and crushes you to rancid jelly you won't catch me losing any sleep over it so stick that one up your bearskin.'

'Wrong way,' hissed Stilts in horror, reaching across and twisting it back to the middle for safety.

A radiant smile spread slowly across Faustulus's Ma's face, like sunrise through the chemical haze over a toxic waste tip. One or two teeth showed through a gap in her beard.

'A real man at last,' she wheezed. 'I like you. You know how to treat a woman properly.' She blinked short-sightedly at the wolf. 'Is that your dog? I must say it's got bloody ugly puppies. I'd drown them if I were you. Come up to the village for some dinner. We'll put on a bit of a feast. Might even invite some of the Sabine women over. They're a bit of a laugh.'

'What's your village called, madam?' said Leonardo.

'Home.'

'Oh well, that's nearly right.'

'You can't miss it. There's no place like it. It's just up the path. Follow the smell.'

Dinner was not a pleasant meal. Trafalgar and Stilts had already had quite enough experience of primitive village life from their visit to Olvis's squalid collection of huts during the first time trip. The only real difference they could see between Ma's village and Olvis's was that Ma's had a better class of tomb. In Olvis's village, the words 'corpse' and 'dogmeat' had been interchangeable but here the back of the village led to a field on the next hill full of rather finely carved stone boxes.

'Etruscans,' muttered Leonardo, looking at them. 'That proves they've got some good stone masons here. I wonder.' A far-away look came into his eyes.

Books had not of course been invented but if they had been, there would never have been much demand for a 'Ma's Riverside Café' cookbook. The directions for the meal they ate would have read 'Strangle your sickest quadruped. Stuff it with firewood. Throw it on the fire until it explodes then search the undergrowth for the scorched bits.'

Leonardo was carefully trying to pick the splinters out of his lump. 'By Jupiter, this is a remarkable dish, madam.'

'It's a recipe my great-granddad brought back from the war.'

'What's it called?'

'He called it Trojan Horse.'

Stilts and Trafalgar found it safest to huddle under the table out of the way of the villagers' huge and clumsy feet. They had other things on their mind. It had seemed a good idea to leave as soon as possible but Daisy had flatly refused.

'They don't have a clue about child care here,' she said when they gave her back a transplug. 'I'm not leaving these two. They'll be dead in no time.'

'Daisy could stay and we could go,' Stilts suggested.

Trafalgar was very unhappy at the idea. 'Anything might happen to her,' he objected. 'The minute Ma realises she's a wolf, they'll have *her* for dinner. Then what?'

'You're not suggesting we stay here, surely?'

It was not a pleasant thought but it turned out to be exactly what Leonardo had in mind when they talked to him after the feast. Ma's tribe was mostly male and they were getting a bit overexcited with the Sabine women so no one was taking much notice of the visitors. Luckily for Leonardo, Ma herself had gone to sleep without taking her helmet off, snoring so loudly and rhythmically that the village musicians were using her as percussion and improvising some rather impressive dance music.

'This is an extraordinary opportunity,' he said. 'It wouldn't take that long, you know. My temple to Mars could be the inspiration that lays the foundations for the most beautiful city ever built. They seem to have all the skills here. They just don't know how to use them. Eat your heart out, Michelangelo. I'll show you who's the best.'

The following day, teams of men appeared at Ma's bidding and, with Leonardo passing instructions through Faustulus, began clearing a large flat area on the side of the hill. Daisy seemed to be taking an active interest whenever the twins went to sleep and when she dragged the anti-gravity sledge out of the reeds and told Leonardo how it worked, the business of hauling boulders out of the way speeded up enormously.

Trafalgar and Stilts took refuge inside the rock and watched them through the one-way windows.

'It's still going to take bloody ages,' said Trafalgar wearily.

Stilts was looking thoughtful. 'Not necessarily,' he said, looking at the screen. 'I might be able to do something about that.'

Leonardo was showing Daisy just how he wanted the foundations marked out when he happened to glance at the rock. There was a faint purple haze around it and, right in front of his eyes, it suddenly shimmered and faded so that a faint, nearly transparent shadow of itself now hung in the air where it had been. Daisy looked up and whined.

TEN

Leonardo and Daisy approached what was left of the rock cautiously. The air became colder as they got close. The artist peered at it. He couldn't exactly see *through* it and yet he couldn't exactly *see* it, either. Its surface seemed indistinct, as if it couldn't quite be bothered to *be* properly. Leonardo prided himself on his knowledge of the behaviour of light but this was so far outside the laws of optics that it deserved a light prison sentence as a deterrent to any other object which might decide to behave in a similar way. He was about to reach for where the door handle was, more or less, when he saw an ant walk busily across the grass at his feet and start to climb the rock. As soon as all its feet had left the ground, it froze into apparent immobility and became just as hard to focus on as the rock itself. He stepped back rather rapidly and decided to leave well alone.

Daisy had an advantage over Leonardo. Being less well educated, she was more able to accept the evidence of her own eyes. They told her the rock was still there and her keen sense of smell told her, even through the closed door, that Stilts and Trafalgar were still inside though in a watered-down form.

Up to this point, nothing particularly dramatic had happened inside the rock. Stilts had had the outline of what might prove to be a good idea. He had been toying with the theory that he might be able to speed up time locally and get Rome built quickly. With that in mind, he'd been playing with the keyboard again. He'd been wondering for a while now what would happen if he clicked the other box on the 'fine tuning' screen – the one that said 'slow' rather than 'fast'. Because nobody had one of the bracelets on, he thought it wouldn't matter. A little bit of his common sense told him it wasn't a good idea to play around with things he didn't fully understand but a bigger bit of his inquisitiveness made a rather disrespectful mental gesture to his common sense.

He clicked it.

He had of course failed to read paragraph forty-eight stroke thirty-two on page 3217 of the manual. This wasn't his fault, because the manual hadn't come with the machine, but in any case no one else had ever got past page eight and, as with every other piece of electronic machinery in the history of electronics, almost everybody groped their way around it by clicking things at random and then doing their best to deal with the unfortunate consequences, usually by turning it off and starting again.

In this case the consequences were not the sort of thing you could turn off. Because all the bracelets were *inside* the rock, Stilts's command affected the whole rock. Furthermore the power calibration of the bracelets depended on the body mass of whoever was wearing one and because nobody *was* wearing one, the effect was to slam the rock and its contents into 'maximum slow'.

As mistakes go, it was not a small one.

The first thing they both noticed was the flickering violet light coming in from outside. The next was that when they looked out through the windows, the landscape was changing rather fast. Opposite them, a stone wall grew all by itself without, it appeared, the help of any human hands at all. As every second passed, it got harder to see out. Insects of all sorts seemed to be rushing to hurl themselves on to the outside of the windows. Through the mass of legs, bodies and wings they could see columns climbing gradually into the air and fantastic carvings spreading along a frieze on top of them. Wooden beams flicked into view, spanning the roof, and were then covered in with stone tiles. Then the layer of insects on the outside of the windows shut out their view entirely.

All this happened in the time it took for them to take in what they were looking at and as Trafalgar shouted, 'Stop it, now!' Stilts was already diving for the keyboard.

As it stopped, even more bewildering things happened. Most of the insects flew, jumped or scuttled away and things they had not previously been able to see jerked into view outside. There were men up ladders and more men hacking away with chisels. Faustulus was guiding the anti-gravity sledge along with a large block of stone balanced on it. Leonardo was scratching calculations on a slate, peering at a piece of knotted string he seemed to be using as a measure. Daisy was in the midst of it, too, keeping one eye on two fine toddlers who were playing in a makeshift pen while she squinted along a wall checking for straightness, urging the masons on with happy tail-wagging, then rushed across to the other side of the building to slink up a ladder growling and scratching disapprovingly at a slate that hadn't been laid properly.

As the mass of insects rose into the air, everyone outside stopped what they were doing and turned to stare. Trafalgar and Stilts stared at each other in amazement then they opened the door and stepped outside.

'You've returned!' said Leonardo, swatting mosquitoes away. 'Well, well.'

'We never went away,' said Trafalgar, feeling explanations were best avoided.

'We saw the rock hadn't completely gone,' said Leonardo. 'I observed that the insects on the surface were moving extremely slowly so I surmised that . . .'

Daisy cocked her head and gave him a hard look.

'. . . that is Daisy and I worked out that . . .'

She growled menacingly.

'. . . that is Daisy told me it might mean the rock was travelling more slowly in time than we were. She said it was probably all right but we'd better not try to explain it to the tribe.'

'What are they doing?' said Stilts in surprise. The whole of the workforce had put their tools down and were kneeling with their foreheads on the ground, chanting.

Leonardo put his slate down and looked embarrassed.

'Ah, well now. It's a long story. It's a bit hard to explain. I've sort of made you into . . . well, gods really, I suppose you might say. It seemed easier that way.'

'Gods!' Trafalgar cried in horror. 'Why?'

'They needed them. I've never come across such a muddled lot in my entire life. Do you know none of them had any idea at all about their own religion and culture? The most remarkable set of deities since the Greeks and *they didn't have a clue*? I've had to start from scratch and take them through the whole thing.'

'Oh dear,' said Trafalgar, 'I'm sure that's not the way it's supposed to work. You'd better tell us what you've done.'

'Well of course, there's Mars. That was obvious. I think Ma's quite enjoying being the God of War. She's grown her beard longer specially. Then you two are Mercury and Saturn.'

'What does that make us gods of?' said Stilts warily.

'Well, Saturn – that's you by the way – is sort of borrowed from the Greek god Chronus. That makes you God of Time, you see? Oh yes, and you keep an eye on agriculture as well.'

'And me?' said Trafalgar.

'You're Mercury. That's like the Greeks' Hermes. You're the messenger of the gods.'

'Oh great,' said Trafalgar, 'Stilts is a god and I'm just a messenger. That's hardly fair.'

'No, no,' said Leonardo quickly. 'It's an important job. Mercury counts as a proper god. You get all the same perks, everlasting life, as much ambrosia as you can eat and all that. Mercury taught the art of interpreting foreign languages, you see. That's what made me think of it. Quite clever, really.'

'Anything else?'

'There's the rock.'

'You're not telling me you've made the rock into a god?'

'No. Not exactly. I've told them it's Mount Olympus, where the gods *live*. It was the best way of keeping them at a safe distance.'

'Isn't it a bit small for a mountain?'

'I suppose you could say that, but they're not very bright you know.'

'Hang on a minute,' Stilts broke in, 'you've left out somebody, haven't you?'

Leonardo looked a bit evasive. 'Who do you mean?' he said casually.

'You.'

'Me?'

'Yes. Which god are you?'

'Er, Jupiter,' said Leonardo quickly. 'Now let me show you what we've been building down here by the . . .'

'This Jupiter,' said Trafalgar. 'He wouldn't happen to be the top god or anything like that, would he?'

'Ah! Well, funnily enough, yes, in a sense.'

'The boss of all the other gods?'

'Look, I had to do it,' said Leonardo, bending down so he could whisper. 'That woman was getting impossible, I tell you.'

'Ma?'

'Yes, Ma. She seemed to think she and I . . . well, you know. She wanted us to . . . Anyway, Jupiter is Mars's *father*, you see. It seemed the best way out.'

They looked at the completed temple to Mars in front of them.

'You're not by any chance building a temple to Jupiter as well, are you?' Trafalgar enquired.

'Oh, how did you guess? Yes, funnily enough, we are. Come and have a look. It's on the Capitoline Hill. It's already half finished. Hercules is a wonderful thing when it comes to doing some quick building.'

'Hercules?'

'Yes, that's what I call that strange contraption of Daisy's. The one that carries the stones around for us. Hercules was very strong, you see – in the legend?'

'Right. So, you've told them the legend?'

'Yes.'

'So . . . the legend that gets passed down through the ages is the one you've just told them here?'

'That's the one.'

'But you only know it because it got passed down?'

'What are you trying to say?'

'I'm trying to say have you started having any headaches?'

Leonardo gave him a strange look and decided to change the subject. 'I've got that piazza thing really worked out now.'

'What piazza thing?'

'The dough with the cheese and stuff.'

'That's pizza, not piazza.'

'Oh *pizza*,' said Leonardo. 'Good. That's much more convenient. We've been getting into terrible confusions. Daisy kept telling me they needed a fountain in the middle.'

Stilts's stomach rumbled loudly.

'Are you hungry?' said Leonardo. 'Come on up. I'm sure they'll have one cooking.'

They walked up the path to the top of the hill and looked around them at a transformed landscape. The village was still there but around it the hill and the next one along had been cleared of undergrowth. Pegs and long lengths of rough twine marked out squares, rectangles and straight lines as far as the eye could see.

'That's the Forum down there,' said Leonardo, 'and we're starting on the city wall next.'

The people they passed kept prostrating themselves on the ground, which made it rather difficult to get anywhere fast.

'I'm not sure I like being a god,' Stilts whispered. 'I might announce my retirement.'

'I don't think you can do that.'

'I don't see why not. Gods can do anything.'

Wafts of delicious cooking smells had already reached them before they got to the centre of the village and found a big new open-plan wooden hut. It had an oven in the middle and Ma was sitting at one of the tables holding a pizza in both hands and trying her best to get it all into her mouth in one go.

'Jupiter!' she cried. 'Who you got there then? That ain't Herpes and Murky thingy, is it? Well, blimey, so it is. Come back then, have they?' She beamed at them with even fewer teeth than before. 'Bin legging it round the heavens for us gods, I bet. Probably hungry.'

Stilts and Trafalgar nodded.

'Soon fix that up,' she said. 'Waiter!'

Four young people, identically clad in red-dyed sheepskins, collided in their eagerness to answer the summons.

'More food,' she said. 'Four more piazzas, quick. Oh yeah, you'd better bring some for these gods here, as well.' She turned back to them, 'They always bring me a plain cheese and tomato when I first get here, just to get the edge off me appetite; that's what they call the Ma Greeter, then I move on to the spicy ones like the Pepper Only. 'Ere, do you fancy a side salad?'

There was a table tipped on its side, draped with ragged clumps of green leaves with a viscous liquid dripping off them. The liquid looked very like wolf saliva.

'Does Daisy bring those?' said Trafalgar, recognising them with distaste.

'Yeah. We can't stop her,' said Ma. 'She gets really cross if we don't eat them.'

'It's doing a roaring trade,' said Leonardo. 'I'm thinking of starting up other branches but there's one or two difficulties.'

'Like what?' Stilts asked.

'Well I'd have to start up the other towns first for them to go in. That's hard work.'

'You'd need a good name, too.'

'Yes. Something with "pizza" in it and "hut".'

'Does anything come to mind?'

'No.'

'No, me neither.'

'Look 'ere, Jupiter,' said Ma suddenly and indistinctly, spraying mozzarella and olives over her audience, 'I'm a bit bothered about this temple of mine.'

'Why's that, Mars?'

139

'It's a bit like, you know, er . . . big.'

'Really? I would have said it had just the right classical proportions, impressive and dignified yet making the best use of its available floor plan.'

'It's just, well, with the old one, when I pulled the door shut it used to touch my knees. It was sort of cosy you might say. I could sit on there for hours and hours like that. This new one looks sort of, well I dunno . . . lonely.'

'Oh you won't be *alone*. There'll be your High Priest for a start and there'll be hundreds of people in there worshipping with you.'

'HUNDREDS OF PEOPLE! Now listen, Jupiter, if you think I'm going to sit in my temple with hundreds of people you've got another think coming. I like to perform my acts of worship ALONE, thank you very much. Bloody disgusting idea. AND it looks draughty. A girl doesn't want a draught round her knees when she's sitting on the khazi halfway through an act of worship.'

It was only then that Leonardo finally understood what she really meant by 'temple' and 'act of worship'. His jaw dropped, then he decided to bluff it out.

'My dear Mars,' he said. 'There must be some mistake. You are a god. Real gods don't need, er . . . khazis. Only humans need that sort of thing.'

'Oh right,' she said quickly. 'No, course not. Er, I didn't mean *me*, no, no, not me. I meant, er, my High Priest. Yes, that's it. My High Priest is going to need a khazi. Just a little one, maybe somewhere round the back, somewhere private where nobody can see.'

There was a short silence.

'Just remind me,' she went on, turning slightly pink. 'This temple thing and the High Priest and that. How does that all work, then?'

By the end of the conversation and a few more pizzas, she rather liked the idea of organised religion.

'Let's go and have a good war, then,' she said. 'Gotta do a bit of godding.'

'You don't really need to start a war,' said Leonardo quickly. 'There'll be plenty coming along. Anyway there's no one around to fight.'

'I dunno,' said Mars. 'There's the Sabine men. They don't like us inviting the Sabine women to all our parties.'

Trafalgar and Stilts had an anxious conversation as soon as they could sneak away to a quiet spot.

'We'd better get him out of here,' said Stilts, looking at the spreading foundations of the new city. 'I'm sure all this stuff isn't meant to be going on.'

'You don't think he's building the wrong city, do you?'

Stilts thought about it for a bit, 'I hope not. But I thought Rome was built in a day. That's the way the saying goes.'

'You've got a point. This is taking much longer.'

'I suppose it must be all right, though. So far everything we've seen proves that you can't change history.'

'No, but you can start it off.'

'Does that matter?'

Trafalgar frowned. 'Matter? What do *you* think? Don't you think legends and gods and things should have slightly more meaningful roots than a bunch of guys wandering in from the future and handing it to them on a plate?'

'OK,' said Stilts, 'I agree. Let's take him back home.'

It proved to be harder than they thought. Leonardo didn't like the idea at all.

'I can't leave *now*,' he said. 'All my life I have studied

141

this city. I know its streets and its buildings like I know my own birth village of Vinci. If I leave now, how can Rome be built properly?'

'How *can't* it be is the question,' said Trafalgar. 'You know how it will be, because you've studied it. There's no choice. That's what it's going to be.'

'I'm not going.'

'You must.'

'Shan't.'

'What about all the things you were doing back home when we picked you up?'

That seemed to get through to him.

'My painting,' he said.

'Was it a special painting?' Trafalgar asked hopefully.

'It is Lisa, the third wife of Francesco del Giocondo,' said Leonardo as if that should mean something. 'I have been working on it for three years. It would be my masterpiece if only . . .'

'If only what?'

'If only she had better teeth.'

'Right,' said Stilts. 'You'll need to get back for that then.'

Leonardo, even though he was the illegitimate son of a rather dull family of lawyers and property owners, was no fool. To be more accurate, he was one of the most intelligent, creative and remarkable people who ever lived. Although time travel was an entirely new concept to him, he had no problems with immediately working out the fine details.

'This thing you have, this rock that leaps the ages, you can control it, yes?'

'Sometimes.'

'So you can take me back to that same spot at that same time?'

'Only if you know exactly when it was.'

Leonardo thought. 'I do. It was the third day of April in the year 1503 and the bells in the Campanile had just rung for the noon-time service.'

'Fine.'

'So that means that we can stay here to build the city because however long we stay here, we can still get back there at the right time, yes?'

Trafalgar groaned inwardly at the thought, then inspiration came to him. 'Yes, but you'll be much older. People will notice.'

'Ah! I see what you mean.'

While Leonardo was pondering this, Stilts leapt in with the decisive argument. 'We could just drop in on Rome on the way back, then you'll be able to see for yourself. It's going to get built the way it gets built regardless.'

'You mean we could see Rome finished?'

'That's right.'

'And if it wasn't right, you'd bring me back here so I could do it properly?'

It didn't seem the moment to start discussing the finer points of the limitations of time travel and the unchangeable nature of history so they just shrugged.

As it turned out, it was one of the worst ideas they ever had.

Then there was Daisy.

She wouldn't even *think* of leaving the twins.

'That Faustulus is fine,' she said, 'but have you met his *wife*? Larentia! I mean to say, is she a slag or what? I wouldn't leave her in charge of a dead toad, let alone the twins. Anyway, I don't trust this lot to build properly if I'm not there keeping an eye on it.' She nodded Trafalgar to one side in a confidential way. 'Leonardo's a great guy,' she said. 'He taught me everything I know, but he's a bit of a traditionalist, you know. There's one or two ideas I've got that I wouldn't mind trying out and it's a good opportunity for me. Normally it's hard for a wolf to make a name for itself in a field like architecture.'

Don't count on getting much credit, Trafalgar thought, but all he said was, 'I'll miss you,' and he stroked her head fondly.

'Well, pop back and see us some time,' she said.

They left her the transplug, feeling she was going to need all the help she could get. Ma insisted on refilling their stores cupboard with fresh pizza, although, because cardboard hadn't yet been invented, they were all stuck one on top of another in a great pile.

'When's a suitable time to aim at?' Trafalgar asked Leonardo as the painter took his seat on top of the rock.

'What about the year zero?' Leonardo suggested.

'That's a good time, is it?'

'Perfect.'

They were just closing the door when he said, 'Be careful where you land though.'

They opened it again. 'What?' said Stilts.

'We'll be right in the middle of the bath-house if we land here.'

'I'm glad you told us. Where shall we go then?'

'I suppose we'd better be somewhere quiet. Let me see.' He jumped down off the roof, looked carefully around him and began pacing off into the distance. He came back looking thoughtful. 'Three hundred paces south-east ought to do it.'

'All right then, here goes,' said Stilts and set the coordinates. They waved goodbye to Ma and Daisy, pushed the button and ran straight into deep trouble.

ELEVEN

It wasn't Leonardo's fault. Three hundred of his paces would indeed have put the rock safely exactly where he intended it to go. He knew very accurately how ancient Rome had been built up over the ages and he had been planning to arrive in a nice quiet bit of undeveloped scrubland just down the hill from the Temple of Cybele. To him, a pace was a pace – not one sixth of a pace. Three hundred of Stilts's paces however, being a lot smaller, didn't get anywhere near the right place.

Offal was a barbarian. At least, that was what the Romans would insist on calling him. *He* didn't think he was a barbarian at all. If anybody had taken the trouble to ask him he would have said he was quite a cultured sort of person, from one of the better tribes in the great gloomy forests of central Europe. His dad had been a Vandal, it was true, but his mother was a Goth and had always insisted they held their knives properly. She was a stickler for that. If you didn't have it just right, with all your fingers and your thumb in the right place, she'd make you start the disembowelling all over again.

Offal had a neat little row of Roman helmets painted on his club to represent the legionaries he'd met and he always kept his face clean and painted. He'd been quite excited when they said he was going to the Circus and even more excited when they said he was going to meet the lion. His Latin wasn't very good at all, so he hadn't understood when they'd added 'in hand-to-hand combat'. It had only started to dawn on him that this wasn't a job with very good career prospects when they'd carried the remains of the previous contestant past him in a basket, leading a very fat lion with a contented expression, which kept belching.

Now, stuck in the compound which served as the Circus waiting room, Offal had started to realise that he'd left it too late to apply for political asylum or Roman citizenship, so he decided it was high time to offer a prayer to his tribe's gods. These weren't the exciting sort. Indeed, barbarians not being known for their vivid imaginations, their gods were mostly rocks, trees and skin conditions. He was very pleased and also quite startled when his prayer was immediately answered. Very suitably, the answer came in the form of an extremely large rock which appeared out of nowhere and flattened a section of the fence round the compound in which they were keeping him. It didn't take him long to decide this was a good moment to leave. He gave his club to the old bloke who was sitting on top of the rock as a thank-you present to Balder, the God of Rocks, and ambled off into down-town Rome to find a good place to wash off the face paint, merge into the crowd and practise his Latin verbs.

For the next thirty seconds, nothing much happened in the compound. Trafalgar, Stilts and Leonardo had forgotten to take painkillers so they were stunned into complete immobility by splitting headaches after the landing. Leonardo had just taken on board the fact that he was now holding an unfamiliar club in his hand when the gates at the end of the compound opened and four guards dressed in the uniform of Roman soldiers marched in to get the barbarian. The guards were not at all happy to find a hole in the fence and a complete absence of barbarian. The Circus Maximus was crammed full with bloodthirsty crowds waiting eagerly for the next event, so losing the afternoon's main attraction was not likely to be greeted as good news. There was a better than even chance that the next event would involve a rapid substitution of guards for barbarians if they didn't come up with something quick. Then they noticed the old bloke holding the barbarian's club.

(Hey you,) one of them said. (Where's the barbarian gone, then?)

(Oh wonderful,) replied Leonardo. (You're speaking proper Latin.)

(No I ain't, I'm speaking Roman, that's what I'm speaking,) said the guard. (You've got a funny accent. Are you a barbarian too?)

(I am from Florence,) said Leonardo, appalled. (I am Leonardo.)

This was an unfortunate thing to say for two reasons. One was that Florence, or 'Firenze' which was what Leonardo actually said, using its Italian name, wasn't going to become well known for another thousand years or so. In the year nought it was simply a sprawl of huts on the River Arno which was known to the Roman guards as 'that sprawl of huts on the River Arno.' The guards thought Firenze definitely had a barbarian sound to it.

The other reason was even more unfortunate.

'Leo' is of course the Latin for 'lion.' Everybody knows that. It is less well known that 'nardo' is Latin for 'fragrant oil from the spikenard plant.' The spikenard was popular among ancient Roman fisherman who tended to use ancient Roman fish as bait when fishing in the Tiber and they had found that spikenard oil came in handy for making the ancient Roman fish smell a bit more interesting to the larger, less ancient and still living Roman fish they were hoping to catch. In effect, then, what Leonardo had inadvertently said to the guards was, 'I am lion-bait.'

It was perhaps not surprising that they burst into coarse giggles and grabbed him by the arms.

(He don't look very barbarianish,) said one of them. (They might not like it. They'll be expecting someone a bit more savage-looking.)

(He's got a barbarian's club.)

(He's not holding it proper. He ought to wave it around a bit more.)

(What he needs,) said the other one, (is some face paint.)

(I am Italian,) said Leonardo desperately. (I am not a barbarian.)

(What's a Tallian when it's at home then?) said one guard.

(It's what you're going to be one day,) said Leonardo, realising his mistake. (I'm a Roman really, just like you.)

There was a chorus of (Oh yeah,) (Make yer mind up,) and (Pull the other one.)

(He'll taste just the same to the lion,) said the head guard. (Lions probably like Tallian food.) He began looking in the puddles for some suitably lurid mud to use as face paint.

Inside the rock, Trafalgar and Stilts watched in alarm as the guards decorated Leonardo's face rather unconvincingly with stripes of mud and then, ignoring his protests, marched him off through the stone gateway in the towering wall of the Circus.

'You don't think they're going to do anything horrible, do you?'

'No, surely not. I expect they're taking him to a party

148

or something. That's why they did that face-painting.'

'Maybe we'd better go and check.'

They peered out through all the windows to make sure nobody could see them, then opened the rock's door and ran across into the shadows by the outer wall of the Circus.

'Come on,' said Trafalgar, 'there's a gap under the door.'

It was a large gap for people their size and they wriggled under it to find themselves in a long stone tunnel with daylight at the far end. They could hear the roars of what sounded like a huge crowd. Inching cautiously along the side wall of the tunnel, they got to the far end and saw a startling sight. There was a huge sandy arena in front of them, with seats banked up all around it. It was packed with spectators and they were all screaming savagely. Leonardo was standing in the middle of the arena, staring wildly around him.

'Do you think he's going to give a lecture or something?' Stilts wondered.

'Possibly. What are they shouting?'

They listened, the transplugs doing their best to filter some sense out of the roaring.

'Sounds like "bring on the lion", as far as I can tell,' said Stilts.

'Oh right. What do you think they want a lion for?'

'Perhaps they think he's tired?'

There were no lions in 95 SEGS, nor indeed were there any other fierce land animals. Once the mice had finished having fun with the datastores during the Sleep, the word 'lion' had come to mean 'inflatable mattress', so Trafalgar and Stilts were both quite surprised when the gate at the far end opened and a huge golden animal with a flowing mane and the sort of teeth that should need an official permit bounded into the far

149

end of the arena and stood there roaring and growling horribly.

'My goodness, what's that?' said Stilts.

Trafalgar tried to remember what he'd learnt of pre-Sleep zoology. 'It could be a Dangeroo,' he said.

'Is it dangerous?'

'Only if there's more than one.'

'You don't think it's another of those ferocious carnival things?'

'I think the term is "voracious carnivore".'

'Well, is it?'

'I don't know, but at a guess I wouldn't say it looked terribly friendly.'

Leonardo knew exactly what it was. He did what came naturally and tried to run away as the crowd rose to its feet and booed him. The lion also did what came naturally and bounded after him, then it knocked him down.

Then it ate him.

Back in the rock, horrified by what they'd just seen, Trafalgar and Stilts tried to be calm and rational about it. They failed. They tried gibbering at each other and managed that a bit more successfully.

'That was *horrible*.'

'What shall we do?'

'We can't do anything.'

'We must.'

'What?'

'I don't know.'

'That was *horrible*.'

That went on for some time, and then they began to calm down.

'I didn't know Dangeroos *did* that sort of thing,' said Stilts. 'Do you think it matters? I mean, as a paradox?'

'Someone being killed fifteen hundred years before

they were born? From the way my head's aching, I suspect it probably does.'

'I mean, it would all depend on whether he was due to do anything that matters in the future, wouldn't it?'

'Suppose he's got a family?'

'If he didn't have a family,' said Stilts hopefully, 'and if he wasn't anybody *important*, then of course it would still be very sad and horrible and all that but it wouldn't really matter, would it? I mean not in terms of time paradoxes.'

'If we could get into the datastores, we could easily find out.'

They tried again. It still needed a password.

'How *stupid*,' Stilts wailed. 'The bloody man goes to all the trouble to fix us up with the rock and everything and then he forgets to tell us the password.'

'Hold on,' said Trafalgar, feeling mildly affronted. 'That's *me* you're talking about.'

'Oh sorry. I didn't mean to be rude. It's not you *now*, though, is it? It's you in the future and for all I know you might have turned into a complete dork by then.'

'That still feels rude.'

'Well, I'm sorry, but you've got to admit it's a bit dumb, isn't it? There's stuff we really need to know and we can't get at it.'

'I'm sure I had a good reason. You know what happened last time.'

They both lapsed into silence remembering the awful consequences to the TS *Titanic* and its crew when Bluto O'Barron had checked the database, refused to believe the accurate version of events he had found there and replaced the entire thing by the mouse-corrupted garbage he was used to.

'Yes,' said Trafalgar, 'but you would have thought I would have fixed it so *I'd* be able to get at it.'

'Perhaps you did.'

'What do you mean?'

'Try typing in your name.'

That didn't work. The screen said 'Access refused'. They tried all the other obvious possibilities, birthdays and so forth. It kept saying the same thing, then Trafalgar, losing heart, tried typing in 'Anya'. The screen said, 'Ha Ha, you sad little man.'

'I'm not doing this any more,' he said crossly, 'not if I'm just going to be rude to myself. Ooh, I'll give myself a good talking to when I get to that age.'

'Hang on,' said Stilts with a sudden faraway look in his eyes. 'What did you just say?'

'I said I'll give myself a good talking to when . . .'

'That's it! All you've got to do is pick a password now and remember to tell yourself later on so that will be the word you use when you set the machine.'

'What shall I choose?'

'Something you won't forget.'

'I don't know how long I'll have to remember it for. I might forget anything.'

'All right. How about "password"?'

'You mean use "password" as the password? That's just silly.'

'No it's not. Try it.'

It worked.

They got into the datastore just like that. The main index page opened up before their eyes. Trafalgar gasped in wonder. Ever since that first priceless uncorrupted datastore had been so briefly available to him before their first trip, he had been bitterly regretting its loss. As a professional historian, there was so much he wanted to know about the true history of the past. Now here it was again, millions upon millions of fascinating items of factual evidence of the way the past had really been before the Sleep and before the mice. There it all was just waiting for him to start exploring it and really, they had all the time in the world. They could just sit there while he read through it to his heart's content and . . .

A new message popped up on the screen. 'No you can't,' it said.

'Oh what?' he cried. 'Why not?'

'Because it's bad for you,' said a further message. 'For your own good, access to non-essential items has been barred.'

'Why's he done that?' said Trafalgar furiously. 'How dare he? The arrogant little . . .'

'Don't talk about yourself that way,' said another message. 'Get on with it. You don't yet understand just how bad time paradoxes can get.'

'See what it says about Leonardo,' Stilts suggested.

'He's right,' said the screen.

'Shan't,' said Trafalgar sulkily. 'I'll do what *I* want to do. Anyway, he won't be in the datastores. They haven't got space for everyone who ever lived, you know. Coming from all that time ago, I doubt they'll even mention him.'

The screen gave a little shiver and filled with information anyway.

'Oh dear,' said Stilts.

Trafalgar was refusing to look.

'What's the matter?' he said.

'I think you could safely say he used to be quite famous,' said Stilts.

'Oh really? Why?'

Stilts read rapidly through it. 'In a nutshell,' he said, 'he seems to have been one of the world's best painters and sculptors.'

Trafalgar tried to shrug it off. 'There's loads of artists. They're always claiming to be the best.'

'Yes,' said Stilts doubtfully, 'but he also invented the diving suit and the helicopter. He discovered how the moon affects the tides. He designed cannons and cata- pults and bridges. Oh look, he was an architect, too. It says he was an expert on the buildings of ancient Rome.'

'Ha!' said Trafalgar. 'Well he would be, wouldn't he? I mean it wouldn't exactly be difficult. After all he built them in the first place. What a cheat.'

'Stop being so sour. It's not his fault we got him eaten.'

'Well, it's not ours either,' Trafalgar brightened. 'Maybe it doesn't matter. I mean perhaps he just dis- appeared in 1506 after he'd done all that.'

'Er, no,' said Stilts, looking at the screen again. 'He died in 1519.'

'That could be a mistake, couldn't it?' said Trafalgar desperately. 'They might have got that wrong. You could easily get something like that wrong, I reckon.'

'I don't think so,' said Stilts. The screen was now showing a drawing of an old man with bushy eyebrows and a long flowing beard. It was definitely Leonardo but it was also definitely older than the Leonardo who'd just been eaten by the lion.

The caption underneath said, 'Self-portrait. 1513.'

'That's not fair,' said Trafalgar. 'That's just NOT FAIR.'

There was a sudden loud scraping noise from outside and the rock lurched wildly.

TWELVE

The dimensions of the disaster revealed to Trafalgar and Stilts by the screen's potted biography of the recently-deceased Leonardo da Vinci had occupied their complete attention and prevented them from noticing what had been going on outside the windows. The rock, having seriously damaged the fence around the Circus stockade and allowed the barbarian to escape, was not, from the point of view of the Circus guards, in an ideal position. It was completely beyond them to understand how it had got there in the first place, but their first task was to get it to go somewhere else so that they could rebuild the fence and make it barbarian-proof again. A whole troop of guards had arrived while the two inside had been discussing Leonardo's life and they were now busy trying to shift the rock with levers, ropes and anything else they could get their hands on.

Being hollow, the rock was lighter than its appearance suggested so the guards found they could tilt it up on one side surprisingly easily. Being macho, unintelligent types, they put this down to their amazing strength and failed to show any sign of curiosity about the unusual lack of density of this particular rock. This saved a great deal of potential trouble. Then it was just a matter of sliding logs underneath it to use as rollers and hauling it through the gap in the fence out of the way. Trafalgar picked himself up from the floor when this rather violent ride was over and watched through the window as the guards hammered stakes into the ground outside to repair their fence. His headache was getting worse and worse.

A groan from Stilts showed he was having the same problem. The guards finished the job and left, leaving nothing much to see in that direction except the repaired fence which they were now outside and the walls of the Circus rising beyond it. When they looked out of the other side of the rock, they got their first clue as to the reason for the extra pain. They had been dumped beside a track in a small patch of rocky ground. The ruin of an older stone building stood a few yards away.

'That looks familiar,' said Trafalgar.

'It's Ma's temple, isn't it?'

'So it is. It hasn't lasted very well, has it?'

'Be fair. It's been a few hundred years.'

'All the same, I'm glad Leonardo didn't see that. He'd be most upset.'

'Not as upset as he'd be feeling if he knew *why* he couldn't see it.'

'All right, all right, I know.'

'It seems to me that we're going to have to do something,' said Stilts 'because we can't just go away and leave it like it is.'

'What sort of something?'

'A rescuing sort of something.'

'How? If it's happened, it's happened.'

'But it hasn't happened, has it? The datastores say he painted his self-portrait. I don't believe anyone has ever painted a self-portrait from inside a Dangeroo's stomach, fifteen hundred years earlier. Therefore, being strictly logical, I would say we've got to do something about it.'

A fierce spasm hit them both. Trafalgar rubbed his head hard.

'These headaches seem to support your case,' he said.

Stilts stared out of the window.

'I've got a feeling that might be something to do with it, too,' he said.

'What?' said Trafalgar, looking where Stilts was pointing, then, 'Oh,' when he saw.

Anyone who has studied a rock will know that there are infinite variations on the theme of 'rock.' Search hard until you find two carefully matched rocks and put them side by side and they will still be found to differ in a thousand ways. The odds against there being another rock a few yards away that looked exactly like theirs were extremely high. The odds against there being a third rock, again exactly like the other two a few yards beyond *that* one, were astronomical.

There was a dried-up old bush next to the furthest one. As they watched, it burst into flames and the rock abruptly disappeared. It was followed a moment later by the nearer rock. Their headaches subsided with them. All that was left to persuade them it had been no hallucination was the burning bush and a trail of smoke leading towards the Circus where the grass was smouldering.

'Oh fine,' said Stilts. 'Brilliant. Now I suppose we're meant to work out from *that* what we've got to do. Great.'

'OK.'

'What do you mean, OK?'

'Let's do it.'

'Do what?'

'Work it out.'

There was a silence. Then there was another silence.

'Haven't you done it yet?' said Trafalgar as a third silence started.

'Me? What about you?'

'You're better at this sort of thing than I am.'

'I can't think of *anything*.'

'These windows are getting really dirty,' said Trafalgar. 'It's all that dust outside.'

'Well,' said Stilts with more than a trace of sarcasm, 'you'd better put it through the nearest rock-wash, hadn't you? I'll bet they've got those everywhere in ancient Rome for passing time travellers. It really doesn't matter, does it?'

'I think it does,' said Trafalgar primly. 'I can hardly see out of this one. Someone's been writing all over it with their finger. Oh . . .'

The message on the outside of the one-way glass was written back to front so they could read it.

The message said, 'Go to "next destination." Get out quickly. Look up. Catch it. Come back here.'

They landed back almost in their own time. It was 80 SEGS according to the screen. They were on a flat rock next to a river at the bottom of a cliff.

Opening the door, they scrambled out.

'I know where this is,' said Trafalgar in delight. 'I used to come here when I was a kid. I got in terrible trouble for . . .'

Stilts was paying little attention. He was staring up in the air and he suddenly sprang towards Trafalgar, knocking him backwards into the rock. When Trafalgar picked himself up off the floor, the door was shut again and Stilts was pushing buttons on the controls. The usual vertigo of time travel shoved them violently back to Rome again and they looked out of the window to find themselves now a little to one side of where they'd been before. There was an identical rock immediately beyond them but just an empty space on the other side. They could see a bit of the first rock sticking through the compound fence and Leonardo's head poking over the top. As they watched, a savage-looking man, dressed in wolfskins and with a painted face, climbed out of the compound, looked warily around him and ran off up the track.

'Hmm,' said Stilts. 'All I did was press "next destination" again. It was already set.'

'We've gone back a little while. This must be just as we arrived first time.'

'Now, let me guess. I've got a funny feeling I know something about your childhood that you've never told me.' Stilts turned away from the controls.

'When you were a kid, you got in terrible trouble for dropping a video camera off the top of a cliff, right?'

'How do you know that? I've never told anyone that story,' said Trafalgar in surprise.

'No,' said Stilts. 'Am I right in thinking you were, let me see, about nine years old at the time?'

'Yes.'

'And the camera was a Kellogs-Benz 911?'

'How could you possibly know that?'

'Because I just caught it,' said Stilts bringing it out from behind his back with a triumphant air.

'That's it!' said Trafalgar. 'That's our camera. My dad was really cross about that. So I didn't break it after all.'

'Only because I caught it. How did you come to drop it?'

Trafalgar thought back to all those years ago when he was a child and they'd gone for a picnic at the cliffs overlooking Rising Gorge.

'My dad said I could use it if I was really, really careful so I was holding on to it very tightly and . . .'

'And what?'

'He never believed me. Nobody did.'

'What didn't he believe?'

159

It suddenly came back to him – the repressed far-off memory of the story he'd told his father, a story which had got him into even worse trouble than dropping the camera in the first place.

'I saw two people get out of a rock,' he said in wonder, 'and it surprised me so much I dropped the camera. Then they disappeared so I couldn't show my dad.'

'I see,' said Stilts. 'It makes sense. I suppose that's how you knew where to go to get your hands on one.'

They both looked at it.

'He made me climb all the way down and I couldn't even find the broken bits,' said Trafalgar. 'Bloody hell. Anyway, now we've got it, what do you suppose we're meant to do with it?'

'Logic would suggest we're meant to use it to film something that's about to happen.'

'The only thing that's about to happen is that Leonardo is about to get eaten. I'm not sure I want to see *that* again.'

'I think we have to.'

They couldn't go in the same way as they went before because they already knew they hadn't been there. Creeping along the outside of the fence, they heard the guards shouting at Leonardo and the slosh of the mud going on his face.

'Come on,' said Stilts, 'there's no time to lose. He's going to get eaten in a minute.'

'I know. I can't find a way in.'

'There must be one, otherwise why would you go to all this trouble to get the camera for us?' said Stilts logically.

'What we need is directions. I wish I'd done something helpful, like drawing an arrow in the dust.'

'You mean like this one?'

They followed the arrows which led them to a drain,

too small for Romans but fine for those who were only a foot tall in Roman terms.

Squirming through it, they found it came out at ground level right on the edge of the arena and there was Leonardo out in the middle of the sand. Trafalgar switched the camera on and started filming.

'Euugh,' he said as the beast did its business. 'Poor old man.'

Stilts was impatient. 'Come along,' he said. 'Back to the rock. We've got to work out what this is all about.'

At that moment there was a small explosion from the far end of the arena, and a large puff of smoke. They made their escape while the crowd was distracted.

The Kelloggs-Benz 911, like all video cameras of the post-Sleep age, had far more gizmos built in to it than anyone who ever bought one knew how to use. Some unscrupulous camera makers had profited from this phenomenon by listing huge numbers of obscure gadgets their cameras were supposed to have and then writing the instruction manual in such a way that nobody could possibly understand how to use them. This saved them the trouble of fitting the gadgets in the first place. Kelloggs-Benz were a good company, however. Their cameras not only did everything they were supposed to do but the controls were labelled clearly and simply and it was almost impossible to get them wrong. For all that, Trafalgar managed to eject the video cassette twice, get it stuck the wrong way round, switch the whole thing off and write 'XXX&-+?yh' on the subtitling display before he succeeded in replaying what they had shot on the fold-out viewing screen. Then he rewound it too far.

'Look, that's ME,' he said. 'Don't I look tiny? I didn't know my ears stuck out like that. Mind you, that's ages ago.'

'It's ages ahead actually,' said Stilts, 'and they still do. Now get on with it.'

They watched several minutes of the family picnic at Rising Gorge then abruptly, there was the animal and Leonardo. It wasn't any easier watching it for the third time and they didn't see anything they didn't already know about.

'Let's go through it slowly,' said Stilts and selected one-tenth speed on the replay switch. It seemed to Trafalgar that all that happened was that Leonardo got eaten more slowly and even more repulsively but Stilts stiffened, replayed it watching very closely and gave a triumphant 'Yes!'

'Yes what?'

'Didn't you see the flicker?'

'What flicker?'

'I'll show you.' Stilts ran it through again, 'It's coming up. Wait a minute. There!'

Trafalgar looked at it doubtfully. 'It's just been dropped three hundred feet down a gorge. It's not surprising.'

'No, no,' said Stilts, impatiently examining the camera's controls, 'you're missing the point. Ah, here we are.'

In the post-Sleep age, video cameras took fifty frames a second and the Kelloggs-Benz allowed you to view each frame at a time if you really wanted to, or maybe if you suffered from extreme sleeplessness. The first 500 frames showed that Leonardo's ankle and knee action while attempting to sprint left a lot to be desired in athletic terms and that leather-thong sandals and long, flapping tunics weren't likely to catch on as premium-price brand-named sportswear. The next 520 showed that nobody in their right mind would ever try to outrun a Dangeroo and the next fifty-three showed what

162

happened when a Dangeroo pushed you over, ending with Leonardo lying face down in the dirt and the beast opening its mouth ready for the first bite. The one thousand and seventy-fourth frame, however, showed an empty space where Leonardo had been and a drip of saliva in midair, falling from the beast's jaw. That was a bit of a surprise for Trafalgar, but not, it seemed, for Stilts who turned to him, grinning, and said, 'Have you got it yet?'

'He's gone.'

'That's right.'

'But we saw him. We saw him being eaten.'

'You want to see the next frame?'

Leonardo was back again huddled on the ground and the next ten thousand frames certainly weren't something you would want to watch in any detail.

Stilts was still grinning at Trafalgar. 'Well?'

'Er . . .'

'Go on. Think about it.'

'We . . .'

'Yes?'

'We use the fast forward and the bracelets to get him out of there?'

'Yes, yes. Then?'

'Then we put him back again?'

'No! Idiot. How would he do all the rest of those things if we did?'

'We take him back to Italy to finish them all off then we bring him back here again to get eaten?'

'NO! That's a really nasty idea.'

'We er . . . We wait until he dies, then we . . . no, I don't suppose so.'

'Listen, Trafalgar, think hard. Supposing that's not Leonardo that gets eaten?'

'Ah! It's somebody else, right? We go and find

somebody else who looks like Leonardo. I know! It's John with a false beard.'

'Come on! You're not going to let that thing really eat someone are you? Not even John.'

'No, you're right. What then?'

'A dummy. Stuffed with something Dangeroos like eating.'

'Brilliant. What do Dangeroos like eating and where are we going to find enough of it to stuff something that size?'

'I haven't a clue.'

Stilts thought for a moment. 'I don't suppose you got into trouble for anything else when you were little, did you? Anything like, say, losing a huge amount of meat while you were looking at a rock that suddenly appeared?'

'Oh don't be stupid. Of course I didn't. That's absolutely ludicrous.'

'I don't know,' said Stilts, hurt. 'It's not so unlikely. I got into terrible trouble when I let someone steal the school barbecue. You could easily have done something like that.'

'Well I didn't.' Trafalgar thought for a moment. 'What did you just say?'

'I don't even want to talk about it,' said Stilts. 'It may have been a long time ago but it still hurts.'

'No, you must. Think about it. It doesn't have to be something *I* did. That could be it.'

Stilts looked astonished as the idea sank in. 'Could it? I wonder.'

'What happened?'

'I was only eight. It was the day before my seventh birthday. I was told to stay behind and look after the food for the barbecue while they lit the bonfire. One minute it was all there, piled up on the table. The next minute it was gone, just like that. I hardly took my eyes off it.'

'You didn't see us or the rock or anything?'

'No,' said Stilts, trying to remember. 'I went outside, just for a second.'

'Why?'

'Someone called me.'

'Who?'

'There was no one there.'

'That's got to be it. What was the food?'

'Two thousand vegetarian sausages.'

'Anything else you remember?'

'Yes,' said Stilts doubtfully, 'the clothesline was on fire.'

THIRTEEN

At the end of a hectic few minutes, the rock contained twenty catering-size boxes of vegetarian sausages as well as eight tablecloths from the line outside the school laundry, slightly singed by time friction, and a number of other items which the speeding Trafalgar had grabbed along the way. Back in Rome again, now occupying the third and final position in the line of rocks, though the other two weren't there yet, Trafalgar was still trying to make Stilts see that they'd had no choice.

'I got into *terrible* trouble for that.'

'It doesn't matter now, does it?'

'It hasn't *happened* yet, that's why.'

'But it will have to happen because it did happen, I mean did have happened.'

'I don't see why you had to call my name. That was a rotten trick.'

'I did have to. You told me. That's what happened. That's why you went outside. Just think how much more of a shock you would have had if the sausages had simply disappeared before your eyes.'

'Well it's all very well for you to say that, but I hope this is worth it.'

'If it saves the life of the greatest artist and thinker in the entire history of the world, then surely it's worth a little inconvenience when you're a kid.'

'A LITTLE INCONVENIENCE! I had to write out "I must not lose the sausages" a thousand times.'

'I'll come back and help you.'

'You can't. I mean you didn't. Anyway how scary do you think *that* would feel? It's traumatic enough already. I blame all my problems with girls on this.'

'Do you?' said Trafalgar with interest.

Stilts looked sulky. 'You're meant to say "what problems with girls?"'

'Oh sorry. What problems with girls?'

'That's not very convincing.'

'Look, just forget it. We have to get a move on.'

'How long have we got?'

They looked out of the window. The fence was still intact. The first rock hadn't arrived yet.

'A while, I suppose.'

The tablecloths were pink, but once they'd rubbed them in the dust they were almost the right colour for Leonardo's arms and legs. Unable to find needles and thread, or rather unable to find thread that didn't burst into flames when he had tried to pick it up at hyper-speed, Trafalgar had settled for a stapler. They ripped up cloth and stapled furiously to make a dummy which would pass for the real thing. The head was a problem but with a lot of trouble Stilts contrived a squidgy sort of pouch which, when it was stuffed with sausages, could just about work.

'I've put lots of ketchup inside, in plastic bags,' Trafalgar said. 'It should look realistic.'

'I don't know about realistic. It needs hair. There was definitely hair in the video.'

They checked and, yes, it certainly needed hair.

'We must be able to find it somewhere,' Trafalgar pointed out, 'because there it is.'

'What about clothes?'

They'd run out of cloth.

'We'll use his own clothes,' Stilts said. 'Look, you can

see the dummy's got them on in the video. It's got his sandals on, too.'

'How are we going to do *that* in the time available?' Trafalgar objected. 'You're saying we've got a fiftieth of a second to get in there, persuade Leonardo to take his clothes off in front of ten thousand people and get out again.'

'It'll be a doddle,' said Stilts airily. 'You won't have any trouble at all.'

'You? You said "you". Don't you mean "we"?'

'Someone's got to stay here and look after the controls.'

'I could do that.'

'You don't know how to.'

'You could show me.'

Stilts looked out of the window. 'No I couldn't. There isn't time. The first rock's just arrived. Now, listen and don't argue. Wear one of the remotes. Take the other one for Leonardo. I'll put you up to maximum speed. You can go straight in the main entrance with the dummy and nobody will notice a thing.'

'How do you know?'

'Because nobody did, did they? We've already been through it. You'd better take a double dose of tablets, though.'

It was quite interesting, stepping out into a normal world then seeing it turn deep red, watching the birds stop apparently dead in midair but not fall down. The dummy, being Leonardo-sized, was a bit of a problem to drag along until Trafalgar found a small wooden handcart and managed to tug the dummy partly on to it so that it was draped over the middle. He trudged round to the main entrance where two guards were standing frozen, blocking the way. They had their legs apart and with a lot of tugging he tried to get the cart and its burden through the gap between them. Its back wheels were wider than the front and when it was nearly through, it stuck fast. Nothing he did could move it so in the end he left it there and hauled the dummy off it and into the arena.

It did occur to him that the guards would be puzzled by the sudden appearance of a wooden cart between their legs, but he had bigger things on his mind. The Dangeroo was frozen in mid-pounce, the drop of saliva hanging in the air. To one side, down by the ground, Trafalgar could see the entrance to the drain where he and Stilts were filming away with the video camera. Over by the entrance tunnel he could see where the two of them were watching events unfold for the first time. It seemed quite funny to think that there were three Trafalgars and two Stiltses in the arena at that moment. He trudged over to Leonardo, hauling the dummy behind him, and had a good look at just how the old man was lying, then he bent down and slipped the second remote on to Leonardo's wrist.

The effect was instantaneous. Leonardo sprang to his feet, stared wildly around and began to run.

'Stop,' shouted Trafalgar. 'Come back. It's all right.'

The artist took no notice. He made it to the far side of the arena before it seemed to strike him that something had changed, then he came to an abrupt halt, looked back at the stationary creature in the middle and noticed Trafalgar.

'Great heavens,' he said. 'Now what have you done?'

'Come back here and I'll show you,' said Trafalgar. 'You've got to take your clothes off.'

A lesser intellect might have balked at the explanation Trafalgar gave him, particularly because Trafalgar didn't really know a great deal about what he was talking about, but Leonardo was Leonardo and the idea of travelling at varying time speeds, already partly familiar to him, was just one more thing for his fertile brain to take apart and analyse. Taking off his clothes in public, however, was something else.

'You can keep your pants on,' said Trafalgar helpfully. 'Believe me, nobody will see.'

'I won't do it.'

'You must.'

'I won't.'

'Well in that case, I'll have to take the dummy away again and you'll just have to be eaten.'

'I'll do it.'

'Good. Put the clothes on the dummy, will you? I've got to go and look for something.'

Trafalgar climbed up through the rows of seated audience, wondering where he could find anything at all that would serve as Leonardo's hair. The audience were an ugly lot and rather a high proportion of them had been caught halfway through picking their noses. There was a special box which looked as though it was for VIPs and in it, surrounded by guards, sat a man and a woman. The man wore a laurel wreath and suffered from a bad skin complaint. The woman had long hair just like Leonardo's. On close inspection it didn't look very convincingly attached to her head. Trafalgar tugged it experimentally and it came away in his hands. Under the wig, she was completely bald. He mumbled an apology and ran back through the crowd to where Leonardo, now dressed only in some rather grey shorts, was kicking the Dangeroo in the ribs as hard as he could.

'Stop it,' Trafalgar gasped, 'that's just childish. Look what I found.'

They put the wig on the dummy's head and stapled two long strands of it together under the chin to look like a beard then Trafalgar adjusted the way it was lying until he was satisfied and they walked back out of the arena past the guards and the cart. Leonardo would insist on staring all around him, not looking where he was going.

'The birds!' he said. 'See the articulation of their pinions! What an opportunity for further study of their musculature!' He staggered into the bush next to the rock.

'Come on, we've got to go.'

Leonardo sat heavily on the rock. Trafalgar took off the remotes, hopped inside the rock and they time-jumped.

Behind them, in normal time, several things happened at once. The bush burst into flames, observed only by the other Trafalgar and Stilts. Rather more seriously, there was a small explosion at the gate of the Circus. This should not have been entirely surprising. As far as Trafalgar was concerned, he had pulled the wooden cart quite slowly for no more than a hundred Roman yards but that wasn't how it seemed from the cart's point of view. In its own time frame it had just covered a hundred yards in about one ten-thousandth of a second, giving it a new land-speed record for wooden carts, had there only been people there to measure it, of about two million miles an hour. As its wheel bearings consisted only of rough holes in the timbers through which its axles passed, it was clear they had never been designed with this sort of speed in mind. In the microsecond immediately following its burst of speed, it heated up instantaneously to several thousand degrees centigrade and exploded into flames.

This was uncomfortable for the two guards between whose legs it was jammed at the time. The puff of smoke and the screams that came from the Circus entrance caused every eye in the huge crowd to swivel in that direction. The spectacle of two guards racing round in circles with their tunics on fire was quite a distraction, so nobody paid too much attention to the lion's behaviour, which was just as well. An experienced observer of lion eating habits might have noticed a certain rather thoughtful expression on its face as it came to terms with the flavour of soya, leek and thyme sausages with ketchup and a scattering of added staples. Nevertheless, it was a hungry lion and it did a very good job. As for the guards whose duty it was to clear away the uneaten bits, it merely confirmed their prejudice that barbarians weren't quite like other people.

At that same second Livia, the wife of Emperor Augustus, felt a disconcerting draught around her head and discovered her wig had gone missing – although anyone in the crowd who mentioned ever afterwards that they'd noticed this fact ran a serious risk of being the main attraction at the very next event.

Stilts was also wearing a remote in case he had to come to their rescue in some way. He had passed the time idly looking through the very few pages of the datastore which weren't barred to him and there he discovered a world map. This looked likely to be useful because it was already marked with every location which the rock, as well as the *Titanic* before it, had been to in their travels so far. He found that moving the arrow to each of the places marked on the map displayed the exact space coordinates of their previous visit to that spot. When Trafalgar arrived back accompanied by an almost-naked Leonardo, who immediately collided with the bush outside, Stilts was just moving the arrow, playing with it.

Trafalgar was highly delighted with how things had

turned out. His headache had completely gone, Leonardo was in one piece and he was pretty sure no one except the Dangeroo would notice the substitution. As Leonardo climbed on the roof, trying to shake bits of burning bush off his legs, Trafalgar rushed into the rock and gave Stilts a hearty slap on the back. The arrow jerked wildly as Stilts's hand clenched inadvertently, pressing several buttons that really shouldn't have been pressed, and the air turned thick and blue as the rock shimmered off to what Stilts had never intended to be its new destination.

It hadn't jumped in time, only in space. It was still the year zero when it landed, and it didn't land very well. Due entirely to Stilts's accident with the controls, it ricocheted off the top of a hill, throwing Leonardo into the middle of a flock of sleeping geese, then it tumbled over and over down the rocky slope. It was a lot further east than Rome so it was now quite dark. Leonardo got painfully to his feet as the geese scattered, honking loudly in all directions. He was covered in a horrid sticky mixture of goose poo and feathers. He looked down the hill and could see no sign of where the rock had got to except that there was a zigzag trail of flames where bits of burning bush had set fire to the undergrowth.

He staggered off in that direction and immediately fell over a small cliff.

The men sitting in the field below were quite startled to see a tall figure covered in feathers plummet out of the sky into the midst of them. They were just finishing their third skinful of good Judaean wine and they weren't expecting a heavenly visitation, especially not one with a beard and feathers. Thinking he was still in Rome, Leonardo addressed them in Latin.

'Excuse me, my friends,' he said, 'will you help me?'

One of the men spoke a bit of Latin. He'd been a Roman galley slave but he'd given it up when he found there was no pension scheme, and escaped. He was very good on the Latin for 'in', 'out', 'faster', 'slower' and 'put your back into it you lazy dog or I'll whip you to within an inch of your life' but the rest of his vocabulary wasn't as extensive as he liked to pretend even when he was sober and he was far from that now.

'Here, where did you come from?' he said.

Leonardo pointed vaguely up the cliff behind him, 'From up there. I am looking for two very small people, friends of mine who are lost. Have you seen them?'

'What's he saying, Ahmed?'

(He says he has come from the heavens above and we must go and search for two babies.)

(He's got feathers.)

(He must be an angel.)

(We'd better do what he says then.)

'Oh magnificent sir,' said the ex-galley slave. 'We shall obey your instructions. Just tell us where to look.'

Leonardo looked down the valley where the bits of burning bush had started some quite major fires by now.

'Go that way,' he said. 'Follow the path of the fires.'

(He says we must follow the bright star to the east.)

'They'll be in a hollow rock.'

(He says they'll be in a cave.)

(Cave?) said one of the others. (The only cave I know round here is that one behind the inn.)

They crashed raucously off down the hill leaving the sheep they'd been looking after bleating behind them to the delight of the local wolf pack.

Leonardo stumbled across Trafalgar and Stilts about half an hour later. They were tidying up the inside of the rock which had come to a stop the right way up in the middle of an olive grove.

'Did a bunch of shepherds find you?' said Leonardo in relief.

'Shepherds? No,' said Trafalgar. 'Three blokes riding great big humpy animals came by and tried to give us some presents.'

'What sort of presents?'

'I don't know. My mother taught me never to accept gifts from strangers.'

'Where did they go?'

'Into that stable over there. I think they're having a party. There's been lots of singing.'

'I'll just go and have a look,' said Leonardo.

'Shall we go and have a look, too?' said Stilts.

'No, it's probably none of our business. We've got important things to do.'

'Like what?'

'Like getting Leonardo back to where he belongs before anything else tries to eat him.'

'That won't be difficult. I found a map. It gives us the exact spot.'

'That's good. What about the time?'

'Leonardo told us, remember? He said it was noon on the third of April 1503.'

The old man came back to the rock with a thoughtful expression.

'Was it interesting?' said Trafalgar politely.

'It's given me a good idea for a picture,' he said slowly.

When Leonardo had told them he knew the precise time the rock had first appeared what he meant was that the clock had just struck noon. To Trafalgar and Stilts that meant it *was* noon. To a sixteenth-century clock, that only meant it was something close enough to noon so that if you decided it was time for lunch you probably wouldn't get in the way of those finishing a late breakfast or starting an early tea. It was, at best, a vague indication of approximate noon-ness.

It should therefore not have come as a great surprise when they returned to Florence, to almost the exact spot where they had picked up Leonardo, to find there was no sign whatsoever of John.

More to the point, so far as Leonardo was concerned, there was no sign of his easel or his nearly-finished painting.

FOURTEEN

Seen from John's point of view, the sequence of events had been extremely disconcerting. Until now he had only experienced time travel from the point of view of a spectator so it was not at all surprising that he was feeling somewhat confused. One minute he had been sitting comfortably on a rock in the year 95 SEGS waiting to be questioned by Minister Lemmon. The next minute he had gone through an unpleasant and unexpected experience in which someone was trying to turn his head inside out by way of his ears and the world rushed at him from all directions at once. No sooner was that over than someone started shouting unpleasant things at him in Italian. He knew just how unpleasant they were because he'd been brought up in that part of New York where they speak as much Italian as they do English, and though these particular insults had an old-fashioned ring to them, they still weren't the sort of thing you expected to hear from a perfect stranger.

He was just sorting out a suitable reply when the perfect stranger punched him hard and knocked him clean off the rock. By the time he had picked himself up off the ground, all there was to be seen of the rock and the man who had attacked him were a few wisps of smoke curling away in the breeze.

By the time he got his breath back, he had to admit that there were a few advantages from the change in his situation. A few moments before he had been by

177

far the largest thing in a miniature landscape and although it had at first seemed quite fun to be regarded as an important expert by Lemmon and the government, he had to admit it was starting to lose its edge. Food was the first problem. They didn't seem to understand that being six times as tall didn't mean that six times the normal portion would keep him going. He had to keep pointing out that he was also six times as wide and six times as deep but whenever he explained the basic mathematics of pizza multiplication, they would get a furtive look on their faces and change the subject. He never had enough.

In addition to that, having to look where he was going all the time to avoid causing serious damage was becoming a problem. The streets of the post-Sleep city which they called London but which he knew perfectly well was New York hadn't been built with someone his size in mind.

The really big drawback looked likely to be his social life. John was a young man in the prime of his life who was inclined to think girlfriends were quite a good idea. So far, the tallest girl he'd seen came to just below his knee – which seemed likely to put a bit of a strain on future relationships. On top of all that they would keep asking him questions about things he knew nothing about, like history. He'd only ever been any good at art at school so he tried to keep them happy for as long as possible by making things up but it was proving a bit of a struggle because they made notes of everything he said and they would keep pointing out the contradictions.

Back in the closing minutes of the old world, it had seemed like a fun idea to change the settings on the sleep pod so that he wouldn't shrink and he wouldn't wake up until Trafalgar's time. Now, he wasn't so sure any more and he was acutely aware that he'd bought a ticket on a one-way trip.

He was therefore amazed, and rather delighted, to find that he was now back in a full-size world, a world indeed that looked as if it came straight out of one of his favourite movies. John was used to the violent, decaying streets of New York in its final days before the Sleep. Until the World President had the bright idea of shrinking everything, an idea born of his first meeting with the time team towards the end of the first blundering, incompetent voyage of the TS *Titanic*, the city had been a vile and lethal place where only the best-protected survived the daily battle to find something or somebody to eat. Escapist movies had been everyone's favourite way of getting through the hungry, horrible days so John had seen plenty of places that looked quite like Hollywood's idea of Florence in 1506. Hollywood, by that time, consisted of an armoured orbiting satellite containing an electronic set of sixty thousand virtual-reality agents, producers and directors who spent all the time failing to return each other's calls and a single rather simple computer which randomly chopped up old movies, rearranged them and beamed them down to the planet below.

Although none of those movie versions of medieval Italy ever *smelt* anything like Florence in 1506, it didn't take John long to decide that this looked a much nicer place than anywhere else he'd been lately.

Warm sun-washed stone buildings with colourfully painted shutters clustered together on both banks of something that was either a narrow river or a wide drain. He was standing in a parched field on the edge of the town. In the middle of the field a picture was perched on an easel. This seemed an unusual thing to find in a field so John walked over to it to take a look and found to his surprise that someone seemed to have nearly finished painting a copy of the Mona Lisa. They'd done everything except the mouth and a tiny bit of the background. There was a palette, brushes and a box of paints on the ground. This looked like fun, John thought. He quite fancied himself as a painter and everyone knew what the Mona Lisa's mouth looked like. Even in the year 2112 it was still on posters, shopping bags and personal protection stun-gun holsters everywhere.

He got it finished in no time and he was just admiring his work when the real thing turned up, shouting at him.

Once again, John's reasonable command of Italian came in handy. He was particularly good on the swearwords which were mostly what she was using.

(Where's that ****, ***** artist?) she shouted. (I knew the old ***** would be out here somewhere hiding.) She was a rather plump woman with fat hands and bad teeth who didn't look nearly as interesting as the portrait made her seem. It cast a new light on the situation and John worked out the implications, came to a frightening conclusion and did a rapid double-take at the picture. If this woman was Lisa, then it followed that what he was looking at was no copy. It had to be the real thing and *he'd* just finished it off. Judging by the complaints she was making it was no wonder they called her Moaner.

(Three ******* years, we've been waiting for that ******* painting,) she bellowed. (He's never going to ******** finish it, is he?) She got to the easel and glared at it.

(Oh,) she said. (He has.)

John didn't think it was the right moment to admit that he'd done it himself. She was standing there staring at it, then she started to, well, sort of twinkle.

(Ooh, I say! *That's* not bad,) she said, (I like the mouth. It's sort of, I don't know. How would you describe it? Mysterious, maybe?)

(Closed?) said John.

(Interesting, I'd say. What's the right word?)

(Enigmatic?)

(Ooh, *that's* a good word. Dunno what it means but it's a good word. Lovely job.)

(Thank you,) said John.

(I'm not praising *you*,) she said sharply. (He did it, the old goat, didn't he? Mind you, you're a good-looking boy,) she said, seeming to take him in suddenly and smiling. This was not a pretty sight. (You remind me of a younger version of that Buonarroti, wotsisname, Michelangelo. You know, the one Leonardo can't stand. You're very like him, you are. You could be his twin brother. Go on then, give us a cuddle.)

He was saved from that horrible fate by a shout from the street on the town side of the field where a short, wildly-overdressed man was standing flailing his arms around.

(Oh ****,) she said, (That's Francesco.)

(Francesco?) John said, relieved, not realising he didn't need the brackets.

(My hubby. Come on, pick up that lot and bring it back to Leonardo's place. That was where we were meant to meet him. I expect he's gone back there, hasn't he?) She called across to the much older man who was waiting for them by the houses, (Coming, dear. You'll never guess what, he's only bleeding finished it, hasn't he?)

(Does that mean I've got to pay the old sod?) came the faint reply.

Art for art's sake has always been a romantic notion.

181

There were a lot of open sewers to navigate on the way to Leonardo's house but when they got there, John decided it was a bit of all right. Painters clearly did pretty well for themselves. There was a big, airy room downstairs filled with odd-looking musical instruments, easels and pictures. Francesco gave the portrait a critical once-over when they were inside. He looked and sounded old, cross and pompous.

(Don't like it,) he said, (not one bit. What do you call that mouth again?)

(Enigmatic,) said Lisa.

(Dunno about that. Looks stupid to me. I may not know about art but I know what I like. No one in their right mind would have that hanging on their wall. I wanted something of real quality. If he thinks I'm paying for that, he's got another think coming. He can keep it as far as I'm concerned.)

He stormed off, taking Lisa with him, moaning again. John looked at the picture and began to worry. He spent a few seconds wondering how he was going to make it up to Leonardo, then, being John and not particularly troubled by a guilty conscience, he got bored with that and stopped wondering. There was a notebook on the table and a quill pen and he began to doodle pictures of his favourite machines, helicopters, bicycles and things like that. After an hour or so he got bored with that too so he went out for a walk and while he was out, something rather unexpected happened to him which had considerable implications for the whole future of art history.

He fell in love.

When Trafalgar and the other two had finished gawping at an empty field, Leonardo suddenly erupted. 'My painting!' he screamed. 'The best portrait in the history of art! Gone! They're expecting delivery today. Three years, that picture's taken me and it's gone! While we've been away someone's stolen it. It's all your fault.'

'John's probably got it somewhere safe,' said Trafalgar, but he knew as he said it that the words 'John' and 'safe' didn't really go together.

'Who's John?' Leonardo wailed so they tried to explain. It didn't even make sense to them and it was definitely a bit too much even for Leonardo to take on board.

'You mean, he's a giant?' said Leonardo in a dazed tone at the end of it.

'Yes. No. He's your size.'

'So he's normal?'

'Yes. No. You'd never call him *normal*, not John.'

'And he's from the future. Like you?'

'No. Yes. He's from *our* past, but *your* future, then he came back with us because in our future he was going to tell the Minister about our past, well that's still your future, which didn't officially happen because . . .'

'Enough!' said Leonardo. 'We'll go to my house and think about what to do next . . .' He shivered suddenly and, looking at himself, realised he was still dressed only in his pants.

'We'd better not let anybody see us,' said Stilts. 'That could cause all kinds of problems.'

'No. Just follow me closely. Do you think *I* want to be seen like this? I knew I should have put on clean underwear.'

The old man led them through a maze of alleys, leaping over sewers and dodging out of sight into the shadows if anyone came by. He helped them climb over the back wall into his garden and they went into the house. Trafalgar saw Leonardo come to an abrupt halt, peer incredulously at a painting on an easel and gasp.

'What is it?' he said.

'It's my painting of La Gioconda. It's here.'

'Oh good.'

'It has been *finished*.'

'Oh good.'

'OH GOOD! Is that all you can say? Three years' work. A breakthrough in artistic technique. An aesthetic dilemma of the first order concerning the expression of the mouth and there it is DONE! FINISHED! Finished by who? Who indeed? Not by me.'

Trafalgar peered at the mouth. 'It's quite interesting, that expression. Enigmatic, you might say. I've seen that picture before, isn't it "The Lost Supper"?'

'NO IT IS NOT. Anyway, that was a mural.'

'And this one isn't Muriel?'

'This is Lisa. Who's Muriel?'

Leonardo went to put some clothes on. While he was out of the room, the front door opened and John walked in with a dreamy expression on his face.

'Hello, you guys,' he said. 'You'll never guess what just happened to me.'

'Don't bother asking what *we've* been doing,' said Stilts sourly. 'Just inventing ancient Rome, rescuing starving children, fighting off wild beasts, developing the pizza and chasing you all over wherever we are, that's all. You just tell us what you've been doing, why don't you.'

'I just met a girl called Maria,' said John, 'and suddenly . . .'

'All right, all right. Cut the cackle. Who is this girl anyway?'

'She thought I was someone else,' said John. 'She rushed up to me and put her arms round me and said . . .'

184

'Michelbloodyangelo. What the bloody hell are you doing here?' burst out Leonardo, coming back into the room.

'Well, that wasn't quite how she put it,' said John. 'She was a bit more polite than that.'

'You're not Michelangelo. You're ten years too young, but you look just like him,' Leonardo added with a puzzled frown.

'That's right. That's exactly what she said next.'

'I'm glad you're not him, I can't stand the bastard.'

'No, no. She said I looked like a younger version of the love of her life and she gave me this big soppy kiss and oooooooooh . . .'

Trafalgar, feeling the conversation was getting into deep water, decided it was time to break in. 'Let's get this straight. You've just been mistaken for someone else, right? Who is this Michael thingy?'

Leonardo looked pleased. 'In the far distant future from which you have come, they have not heard of Michelangelo?' he said.

'No.'

'But they have heard of me, yes? They have heard of Leonardo da Vinci?'

'Oh yes, yes,' Trafalgar said quickly.

'No,' said Stilts, then, 'Yes, yes, yes, ouch,' and started rubbing his ankle hard.

'You haven't heard of his statue, David?'

'My name's Stilts.'

'Fool. The *statue's* called David.'

'Can't say I have.'

'I *knew* it was overrated. What about this new job the Pope's given him? Have you heard about that one? Painting the roof of the Sistine Chapel?'

'Oh, he does decorating too, does he? No, I haven't. Anyway, why do you want to know?'

'He is an upstart. Far too full of himself. I bet he makes a real mess of that roof.'

John, who seemed miles away, started singing softly to himself, 'Maria, Maria . . .'

Leonardo raised his eyes heavenwards, 'Do stop him going on about Maria. She's besotted with Michelangelo. He hasn't got a chance. Anyway what are you going to do with him?'

'That's a bit of a problem.'

'Look. He's written all over my notebook!'

'I'm sorry. He does things like that.'

'I'm hungry,' said Leonardo. 'We could go out for a pizza.'

'Do they have pizza restaurants here then?'

'Well, they didn't when we left but now I've introduced the pizza way back then, they should have it by now, surely. Why are you shaking your head?'

'It doesn't work like that. Nothing you did then will have changed anything now.'

'You mean they've forgotten about pizzas? Am I going to have to invent them all over again?'

'I don't know. Are you famous for inventing the pizza?'

'I could be, I suppose.'

Stilts yawned loudly and Trafalgar felt suddenly deeply weary, as if he hadn't slept for several thousand years, which he hadn't. Leonardo showed them to couches in the next room and then went back to where John was sitting. He stared at the Mona Lisa then at John.

'It's not bad,' he said grudgingly in the end, 'though I think you copied it from me. That smile's just like the one I used in "The Virgin and Saint Anne."'

'Is that a film?' said John but Leonardo only looked at him blankly.

'Anyway,' said Leonardo, picking up the notebook, 'enough of that for now. I want you to tell me all about these machines of yours. What is this thing here?'

'That? That's a sort of helicopter.'

'Is it for cutting corn?'

'No, it's for flying.'

Leonardo took a closer look. 'Wait a minute,' he said. 'That's not new. I invented that years ago – armoured cars, shells. Who are you trying to kid? You've just copied out my old notes.'

'No I didn't,' said John, affronted. Then a cunning look came into John's eyes. He'd been thinking about Maria and the infinite possibilities of time travel.

'I've got loads of other inventions I could show you,' he said. 'I'll do you a deal. I'll give you lots of other ideas but first of all I want to know everything there is to know about this Michelangelo bloke. Especially where he was about ten years ago and what he was doing.'

Trafalgar and Stilts woke after a deep sleep to a fine Florentine morning. They helped each other down off the couch and wandered in to the room next door where Leonardo was making some fine alterations to the background of the portrait.

'You're leaving the smile, then?' observed Trafalgar.

'Yes. That strange friend of yours says he copied it from the way he knew the picture turned out anyway.'

'So who invented it then?'

'I did.'

'When?'

'Do stop being difficult,' said Leonardo crossly. 'What matters is that this portrait of mine will live on into the infinite future.'

Trafalgar didn't like to tell him that, along with almost

every other painting on earth, it was destined to be eaten by the mice during the Sleep and would only survive as a mis-titled screen-saver.

'Right,' he said. 'By the way, where is John?'

'He went off,' said Leonardo vaguely. 'Blast. I've run out of umber.'

'Went off where?'

'I don't know. He left you a note.'

The note didn't say exactly where John had gone off. It did say when, though. He'd gone off to the year 1494 and he'd taken the time machine with him.

FIFTEEN

1492 was a good year for Christopher Columbus, who got a huge amount of credit for getting lost, finding the wrong continent and ruining the next four centuries for the Red Indians. 1492, on the other hand, was a very bad year for Michelangelo Buonarroti. He was seventeen and everything had been going remarkably well until then. He'd hacked out a couple of good sculptures and he'd got in with most of the people who mattered in Florence. The Medici family were *the* people to know at the time. They were the boss family and when it came to dealing with the Medicis, you were definitely either on their side or out there in the cold trying to avoid giving passing assassins a chance to hone the finer points of their professional skills.

For gangland thugs, they had a fine appreciation of art so Michelangelo was in their good books and enjoying himself like a pig in muck. Until 1492. That was when old Lorenzo de' Medici, his main patron, spoilt it all by dying most inconsiderately. Things went from bad to worse after that.

By 1494 everything had got even worse. Politics and violence were fairly interchangeable ideas in those days and Lorenzo's descendants had to run for their lives. Suddenly being in with the Medicis was only slightly preferable to catching plague. One night, Michelangelo had to run with them and he headed out of town in the general direction of Bologna as fast as his feet could carry him. He wasn't very good at running in the dark, not having particularly good night vision, and when a large rock loomed up out of the gloom ahead of him he swerved to miss it and fell straight down a ravine.

John, who was sitting on the rock, was horrified. Manslaughter hadn't been his intention at all. It was the second time he'd used the machine because he'd decided to make a quick trial trip, just to get used to the controls. Stung by Leonardo's declaration that he already knew all about helicopters and all the other machines John had drawn in his notebook, he'd nipped back to 1482 and dropped the notebook off in Leonardo's room just to have the satisfaction of knowing it *had* really all been due to him. After that he'd come up with a vague plan that if he just had a nice chat with Michelangelo, they would see if they could come to some mutually acceptable arrangement by which Michelangelo would see the undeniable sense of swapping identities. He thought he could probably tempt the man by the choice he could offer of delightful places in the future world. He was sure Trafalgar and Stilts wouldn't mind dropping Michelangelo back at some nice peaceful time in the future when there was air conditioning and antibiotics and fast cars, particularly if he got the artist at a good psychological moment.

Once he'd got the date, time and direction of Michelangelo's forced exit from Florence out of Leonardo, the rest had been a doddle. He knew all about computers and, by using a long stick, he was able to reach in through the door of the rock and press the right buttons. It had seemed likely that he'd have to hunt around to find Michelangelo when he arrived at his destination, a little way out of town on the Bologna road. What he hadn't been expecting was to see his double immediately race towards him out of the darkness, running at quite an impressive speed, then turn and plunge into a chasm with a terrible yell. By the time John managed to scramble down to him there wasn't anything much to be done except bury him, which he did.

Still at least that sorted out one problem.

It left Trafalgar and Stilts with a bigger problem. They waited for darkness before venturing out into the streets. The moon was out by the time they got to the field and the rock definitely wasn't there.

Back at Leonardo's, they cross-examined the painter about what he and John had been discussing.

'It's obvious, isn't it?' said Trafalgar in despair. 'He's decided he wants to *be* Michelangelo. He's stolen the rock so that he can go back to try to fix it.'

'Talk about selfish,' said Stilts. 'He could easily just have gone back in it but still left it there in the same place so we'd find it. I wonder where it is?' He looked at Leonardo. 'You don't remember if there used to be a rock in that field a few years ago, do you? Maybe someone hauled it away.'

Leonardo shook his head. 'I don't think so.'

'We're stuck then.'

Trafalgar was thinking hard. 'Suppose John succeeded.'

'How do you mean?'

'Well, just suppose he went back a few years and managed to take Michelangelo's place.'

'Yes?'

'He'd be around *now*, wouldn't he? He'd be Michelangelo now.'

'That's right.'

'And the rock would still be around. He'd know exactly where it was.'

'Aha.'

'Leonardo,' said Trafalgar, 'Do you happen to know

where Michelangelo is now and what he's doing?'

'Of course I do. He's gone off to Rome. Pope Julius thinks the sun shines out of his, well you know what.'

'No,' said Stilts. 'What?'

Leonardo told him.

Stilts was genuinely interested. 'How could the sun do that?' he said.

'I think it's just a figure of speech,' said Trafalgar gently. 'We'd better go and find him, hadn't we?'

'Oh no, not Rome again. Terrible things happen when we go to Rome.'

'It'll be all right this time,' said Trafalgar with totally unjustified optimism.

'How do we get there then? We're a bit noticeable, you must admit.'

John had got into his new role quite quickly, thanks to the rock. He had a definite touch of genius as a painter and if people noticed a slight change in Michelangelo's style after his departure from Florence, they put it down to his increasing maturity and the trauma of exile. The citizens of Bologna noticed how strange his accent sounded, being twenty-second-century New York Italian, but, being intensely suspicious of any outsiders, they were quick to put it down to the fact he'd come from Florence. Anyway, it didn't take him long to start speaking like a native. It was the sculpture that gave him trouble at first. He'd never done any and since Michelangelo was mostly known for his wonderful statue of David, people not unnaturally expected him to be rather good at it.

Inconveniently, it quickly became clear that the real Michelangelo had already taken a big fat fee to do a series of statues for the shrine of San Dominico. It wasn't at all clear where the money had gone but the man who'd ordered them looked like his descendants might turn out to be the Mafia in another four or five hundred years so John thought he'd better have a go at fulfilling the contract. His first attempt with a hammer and chisel gradually reduced a promising block of marble to a floorful of marble chippings and absolutely nothing else. He swept it all up before anyone saw it. The trouble was not only did he not have much of an idea how to sculpt, he also had no idea what the statues were meant to look like.

That was when it struck him that possession of the rock gave him a certain edge and he started to think hard. What happened next was a terrible misuse of time travel and nobody reading this book should *ever* do what he did.

The librarians of the New York Central Library of the year 2100 would have been very surprised to see a large rock materialise next to the enquiry desk if they had been there to see it. John had chosen Christmas Day for his raid, so they weren't there, even though the rock's arrival set off every alarm in the place. It only took him three minutes to raid the library's art section for its full-size hologrammatic replicas of the statues he wanted, though he nearly got caught when he grabbed a book or two as an afterthought. By the time the security guards came storming up the stairs there was nothing to be seen but a thin wisp of smoke.

Back where he started, with the first hologram set up next to a nice new block of stone in his studio, John discovered it still didn't help a great deal. He could now see what it was meant to look like but he couldn't see where he should start chiselling in order to get there.

Until he started working backwards.

He got the block lowered onto the top of the rock then he jumped forward to the finished statue. The whole process, from finish to start, took him three months. He went back one chisel-blow at a time from the final version, looking carefully at where he had to hit it, and then made his move. This removed any chance of a mistake. By the time he'd worked right back to the first blow, gradually seeing the block of stone assemble itself around the statue and the pile of chippings in the floor disappear, he'd learnt a great deal about sculpture. The second statue only needed a little cheating and after that it was a doddle, though he had to keep his doors firmly locked when he was working in case anyone saw what he was doing. When he was called to Rome to do a huge statue of Bacchus, the God of Wine, Women and Song, he was confident enough about his new skills to do it in the normal way, starting at the beginning and going forward, though he did have the photographs from the books he'd stolen to help him out. He was extremely keen to get to Rome, because he had learnt from his cross-examination of Leonardo that it was in Rome that he was fated to meet Maria and that, after all, had been the whole point of the exercise in the first place.

Rome was more of a problem for Trafalgar and Stilts. Leonardo was getting tired of having them around and tended to blame them for the fact that Giocondo refused point-blank to accept delivery of the Mona Lisa. He was starting to behave as though they were a rather unpleasant hallucination and it was clearly time for them to go. The trouble was they couldn't leave the house except under cover of darkness and even then there was always the danger they'd be seen. It was a hundred and fifty-five miles from Florence where they were, to Rome where they needed to be. That was a hundred and fifty-five full-sized miles so for them, being

194

only one sixth of full size, it was more like nine hundred and thirty miles and that was definitely too far to walk.

At five o'clock one morning, prowling through the shadows in the southern part of the city, they came across a cart being loaded up outside a workshop. There were candles burning in the workshop and through holes in the wall they saw a long line of painted statues waiting to be packed.

Two men were carefully wrapping the statues in straw, talking as they worked.

'Two days getting there,' one of them said, 'two days back again. I don't know why I do it. Getting carved up by all the flash gits on the Appian Way. You don't know what it's like. They don't give a toss, those guys in their sports jobs. They'll overtake coming right at you, three abreast. Fifteen miles an hour, some of them do. Makes your hair stand on end.'

'You ain't got any hair, Marco.'

'That's 'cos it got tired of standing on end. Anyway, has that horse had a good feed? I don't want it running out of fuel halfway to Rome.'

Trafalgar and Stilts were across the yard and into the back of the cart in no time flat, burrowing down out of sight into the straw between the statues. When the men put the last of the load on board, they didn't notice a thing.

Six months later, Michelangelo was standing on the scaffolding playing with a few ideas for the very first section of the Sistine Chapel ceiling. It was late in the evening and the doors were locked, which was why he was surprised to hear echoing footsteps coming towards him on the floor below and two people arguing in a way that suggested that this particular argument had been going on for a very long time.

'Yes, but if you hadn't *sneezed* in the first place, they'd never have said it *was* a miracle, would they?'

'You can't blame me. If you hadn't fallen asleep in the cart, we would have known where we were and . . .'

'You fell asleep, too. The first thing I knew was when his hand grabbed my leg. I tell you, I went rigid with fright.'

'Well there you are, if you hadn't gone rigid they'd never have thought you *were* a statue, would they?'

'And what about you? You did exactly the same. Next thing I knew we were both standing there by the altar and they were lighting all those candles and stuff.'

The painter gazed down at two tiny figures, their faces covered in white paint, dressed in long flowing gowns. The gowns had rather charred edges.

'Trafalgar?' he said in wonder. 'Stilts?'

'Saint Dominico to you,' said the nearest one sourly. 'And this is Saint Sebastian.'

'It *is* Trafalgar. What on earth happened to you?'

'I might ask you the same question, John. Nicking our rock like that.'

'Oh, I'm usually called Michelangelo now. Anyway, I'm going to bring the rock back when it's the right time, I mean when I get back to the same time it was when I took it . . .' A worried look came into his eyes. 'Hang on, what year is it?'

'Exactly. We've been trying to find you for *months*.'

'I'm so sorry. Time flies when you're enjoying yourself. I could have sworn it was still 1506.'

'I could have sworn, too.'

'You did,' said the figure dressed as Saint Sebastian next to him, 'often.'

'So did you,' said Trafalgar indignantly. 'Conduct unbecoming a saint, I'd say.' He looked up at John again. 'Do you know what he did? They brought us food

196

and he only went and *ate* it while they were watching.'

'Who did?' said the man, faintly.

'Stilts did. I mean, can you imagine? There we were, trapped inside this church, having to pretend to be plaster statues, right? But at least the children brought food and drink in to put before us, so when they'd gone we could scoff it down. Anyway there we were one day and while they're watching, *while they're watching*, mark you, this twit goes and reaches out for one of the cakes and EATS it.'

'It wasn't my fault,' said Stilts. 'They wouldn't go away and I was so hungry.'

'Well, after that life got unbearable. They were hardly going to leave us in peace after *that*, were they? Wall-to-wall kids staring at us, morning 'til night. Have you ever tried not blinking for twelve hours at a time? We could only eat when it got pitch dark.'

'Couldn't you have got out?'

'With a door like that? It must have been the only door in Italy that reached right down to the ground. Hardly a gap worth mentioning. They locked it up every night, too.'

'You must have had an awful time. I mean how did you . . .'

'There were some difficulties I'd really rather not discuss,' Trafalgar cut in, primly.

Stilts began to giggle. 'Do you remember that time there was only one of them looking? That rude kid?'

Trafalgar looked at him sternly, 'That was nothing to be proud of.'

'Go on,' said Michelangelo, 'what did you do?'

'I stuck my tongue out at him.'

'So?'

'He didn't half yell. He told everybody.'

'He got smacked for it,' said Trafalgar. 'No one believed him. I didn't think that was very nice.'

'He hadn't kept poking *you*, had he? He deserved it, believe me.'

'How come you've got paint all over you?' Michelangelo asked.

'Oh that was VERY funny, I must say. Ho ho ho. They only decided we didn't look saintly enough. It was horrible. It got in everywhere. Of course, they stripped our clothes off. Talk about embarrassing. These stupid robes itch like mad.'

'Well never mind, you're here now. How did you get away?'

'We had to escape,' said Stilts defensively. 'We just had to, once I heard what they were planning to do to me. Do you know about Saint Sebastian?'

'Er . . .'

Stilts's voice took on a solemn tone, 'He was shot full of arrows, that's what happened to him.' He quavered a little. 'They decided I'd look more realistic if I had lots of arrows sticking out of me too.'

'So how did you . . . hang on a minute. This wouldn't by any chance be the Church of San Lorenzo, would it?'

'It might,' said Stilts suspiciously. 'Why?'

'The one that burnt down last night?'

'They could easily have put it out if they'd tried a bit harder.'

'Hang on, are you telling me you started the fire in order to get out?'

'Candles are very dangerous things,' said Stilts. 'They just left them there, burning all over the place. It could have happened at any time. Anyway, what's all this, then?' He waved a hand at the scaffolding and, though Michelangelo suspected for a moment that he was only trying to change the subject, he couldn't resist it.

198

'Come up and have a look,' he said.

They tried to get up on the first rung of the ladder but it was on a level with their heads and anyway their robes kept getting in the way.

'Hang on a minute, I'll lower my bucket down for you.'

It was a wobbly ride up to the top of the scaffolding but when they got there, they were too surprised at the sight of what Michelangelo was painting on the ceiling to worry about it for long.

'Do they *have* women with clothes like that round here?' said Stilts in wonder.

'What clothes?' said Trafalgar. 'I think that's a hand-kerchief.'

'Don't you like it?' asked Michelangelo, hurt.

'Oh yes, I love it. It's just, um . . .'

'What?'

'Isn't this a church of some sort?'

'You don't think it's suitable?'

'Um . . . has anyone else seen it?'

'No, I only painted it tonight.'

'What's that thing behind them with flames coming out of it?'

'That's a hover-tank with a pulse-jet engine and missile launchers.'

There was a long silence.

'I haven't seen any of those round here,' said Trafalgar hesitantly.

'No, of course you haven't. They haven't been invented yet.'

'Don't you think it might be a bit, um, ahead of its time?'

'Art is meant to be ahead of its time,' said Michelangelo pompously. 'Great art should not be shackled by the chains of convention. Let them run to catch up with the fleet-footed, nimble-minded, far-seeing geniuses of the time.'

'That's you, you mean?'

'Well . . . yes.'

'The world might not be quite ready for this.'

'Oh, all right. I'll paint over it. I suppose you think it should look more like this?'

He produced a crumpled photograph of a colourful ceiling covered in biblical figures.

'Oh, really,' said Trafalgar sternly. 'You've been cheating, haven't you? Is this, by any chance, how it ends up?'

'Apparently,' said Michelangelo defiantly. 'That doesn't mean I have to do it, does it?'

'I think it probably does actually. Unless you can put up with the headaches.'

'This time travel business is very bad for originality,' grumbled Michelangelo, 'I will not let it cramp my style. My hover-tank is just as good as this.'

'Oh yes, that reminds me,' Trafalgar said, looking around. 'What *have* you done with the rock?'

'The rock. Ah, yes. I wanted to talk to you about the rock.'

'Talk then.'

'I just wondered . . . I mean I'm sure you . . . that is, you did have it properly insured, didn't you?'

'Why is it that sends shivers down my spine?' said Stilts.

SIXTEEN

'Exactly how badly damaged is it?' said Trafalgar, icily.

'It's just, well, the roof's a bit lower than it used to be.'

'How much lower?'

'Um, quite a lot really.'

'What in the world were you *doing* in 1174 anyway?'

'I needed some more stone for my carving, see?'

'Couldn't you just *buy* it like anyone else would?'

'How could I? I didn't have any money.'

'Why not?'

Michelangelo struck a tragic pose, 'We artists are destined to suffer in poverty for the sake of our art.'

Trafalgar snorted.

'Oh, all right then, I spent it all on Maria if you must know,' Michelangelo said defiantly.

'So what happened?'

'I looked around a bit, you know how it is. I sort of flitted here and there in the old rock. Don't worry, I was behaving myself pretty well. Anyway, in the end, after I'd been looking for a while I happened to come across this big pile of blocks of stone, already neatly cut, just lying there. Absolutely perfect, they were.'

'You happened across them?'

'Yup. All stacked up nicely, just crying out to be used.'

'Where were they?'

'Not far away. Some little town down towards the coast.'

'In 1174.'

'Er, yes.'

'You haven't got a clue how dangerous that sort of thing is, have you? Someone may have to spend *years* sorting out the mess you might have left behind.'

'I was careful, I promise.'

'How come you picked 1174 anyway?'

'My finger slipped. Anyway, it wasn't really my fault. I'd only have been there for a moment, but I was just about to load one of the blocks on to the rock when this really gorgeous girl walked by.'

'Wait a minute. I thought you were supposed to be in love with Maria.'

'Oh, I am, but this was just *after* I went back and so it was a long time *before* I met Maria properly for the first time in the right order, so it's all right, isn't it? I mean to say you can't two-time a girl if it's more than three hundred years before she was born, can you?'

'That's probably rather a complicated moral question.'

'What's a moral question?'

'Something you're probably not too familiar with.'

'Anyway, it's not quite what you think. You see this girl Francesca looked just exactly like Maria.'

'What sort of an excuse is that?'

'Maria says her family came from round there.'

'So you're saying this was Maria's great-great-great-great-great grandmother?'

'Something like that.'

'And that makes it all right?'

Michelangelo put on an innocent look and shrugged. 'You could say it was a sneak preview.'

'Let's get back to the point,' Trafalgar suggested. 'What happened next?'

'I went off for a bit.'

'With Francesca?'

'Yes, and when I came back, they'd built something on top of the rock.'

'What?'

'A campanile.'

'Is that some sort of tent?'

'Well, you could call it a sort of tent, I suppose,' said Michelangelo evasively.

'What is it then?'

'It's more of a bell tower, really.'

'A BELL TOWER? A *stone* bell tower, by any chance?' Trafalgar's tone was distinctly frosty.

'Yes, you could say that. Stone would just about cover it. That's what they'd put the pile of stone there for in the first place.'

'But a *bell tower*? How long were you away for?'

Michelangelo looked a bit evasive, 'I don't know. Maybe a few days?'

'*A bell tower, in a few days*?'

'Well, it depends what you mean by a few.'

'Oh, right. What *do* you mean by a few?'

'Oh I don't know. Say, six months?'

'You went away for six months. You left *our* rock unattended for SIX MONTHS?'

'There's no need to shout. Anyway there's not much harm can come to a rock, really, is there?'

'It would seem harm somehow found a way,' said Trafalgar trying to keep his voice under control. 'So, just to get this absolutely straight, when you finally dragged yourself away from the delights of Francesca they'd built a bell tower on top of our rock?'

'Yes, that's right,' said Michelangelo. 'I was quite surprised – and it was.'

'What was? Was what?'

'Absolutely straight, the bell tower, that is. Well at *that* stage it was, anyway.'

'How did you get it out?'

'They hadn't built it completely on top of the rock, you see. There was only one little tiny edge of the tower actually *resting* on it.'

'All right, all right. What did you do?'

'I had to work all night. It wasn't easy, I tell you. I had to dig a tunnel to get down to it. The tower had sort of pressed it down into the ground. It was really difficult getting the door open.'

'And then?'

'Oh you know, I just had to reach in and reset the controls, then I hung on as hard as I could and pressed the button.'

'And the machine jumped back here?'

'That's right. The only real damage is the roof.'

A thought struck Trafalgar. 'What happened to the tower?'

'The tower? Oh you know, it turned out quite well, really. I mean it's very unusual. There's nothing else quite like it. I think it's quite nice. It's even become a bit of a tourist attraction now. Lots of people go to Pisa just to look at it. I expect they were quite pleased. Once they'd got over being very not pleased, that is.'

'Do they know what caused it?'

'No, they never had a clue.'

'So where's the rock now?'

'I'll take you to it.'

'And all this is what you meant when you'd said you'd been careful?' Michelangelo was silent.

Stilts pointed at the chapel roof, 'Speaking of being careful, don't you think you'd better paint over that lot first?'

The rock was hidden really brilliantly in a pile of rocks. They wouldn't have recognised it. It was a battered ruin of its former self, half the height it had been before and with large chunks of builder's mortar still stuck all over its flattened roof.

'Oh really,' said Stilts crossly. 'You haven't a clue how to look after other people's things, have you?'

'You did say you'd insured it, didn't you?' said Michelangelo innocently.

'No, of course we didn't. When did you last try to insure a time vehicle? "Oh certainly, sir, and exactly what model time machine is it? The GLX or the GTI?" Ha ha.'

'I tell you what. My sculptures go for a lot of money these days. If I signed it, you could probably make a fortune out of it.'

'You've looked yourself up in the books, haven't you?'

'Me? No. Well . . . yes.'

'And do they mention a statue called "Time Machine Flattened by Bell Tower"?'

'Not as such.'

'There you are then.'

The rock's door opened with a series of complaining squeaks and screeches. They had to crouch down to get in and they couldn't even sit upright in the seats any more.

'Are you going off then?' said Michelangelo.

'I can't see much point in staying,' said Trafalgar. 'Look, do promise not to do anything really daft, won't you? Anyway there's no point in trying to. It can't be any other way than it actually was.'

Michelangelo took the photo of the Sistine Chapel ceiling out of his pocket again.

'Oh yes it could. If I wanted to, I could paint absolutely anything I liked up there. I think I'll go back and add some jet fighters to it.'

'You could try,' said Trafalgar, 'but it just wouldn't

come out any other way, plus the fact that the Pope would probably have your ears cut off.'

'So you want me to do it this way? What sort of artist would I be if I simply *copied*?'

'The same sort you already are,' muttered Stilts. 'Here, give me that,' he said more loudly. He ripped the photo into small pieces and threw it away in the wind.

The other two looked at him aghast.

'He wants to be original,' said Stilts, shrugging, 'so let him invent it. If it's going to come out that way, it's going to come out that way, right?'

'Right,' said Trafalgar faintly.

Michelangelo waved them goodbye, watched the rock shimmer out of existence in his time, turned to go and tripped headlong over a bramble. Hitting his head on a small boulder, he plunged into deep unconsciousness and awoke to find his head being bathed by Maria. It was then that his head filled with angels and glorious visions and he had the first of many religious experiences that led him to his great masterpiece on the chapel ceiling . . . either that or maybe the concussion had given him a photographic memory.

'What now?' Stilts had said as they crouched awkwardly in their seats, heads pressed hard against the rock's crushed roof.

'Let's go home, then we can change.'

'Home! Now there's a nice idea.'

'The only thing is . . .'

'. . . we'll have to face Lemmon,' Stilts finished for him.

'We could go home just for an hour or two some time when we know I wasn't there, so we could grab a quick wash and brush-up. Say, midday a couple of days before we left.'

'You might come back unexpectedly and find us.'

'I didn't, did I?'

Stilts thought about it. 'Sounds good to me. Let's go.'

They couldn't.

When they tried it, the machine wouldn't let them.

'WHAT ABOUT THE LAST JOB?' it said in bright red block capitals.

'Oh no,' Trafalgar groaned. 'What does the machine care if I do the jobs or not?'

'IT'S NOT THE MACHINE,' said the screen, 'IT'S ME.'

'Who's ME?' Trafalgar said crossly.

'You,' said Stilts. 'Come on now, we've seen this before. Your future you remembers this conversation so it's programmed the machine with the right answers.'

'THAT'S RIGHT,' said the screen.

'Try and ask something useful so we get some worthwhile information,' Stilts prompted.

'Er, right.' He addressed the screen feeling a little self-conscious. 'Why can't we go home?'

'BECAUSE THERE'S STILL ONE MORE JOB AND IF YOU DON'T DO IT THEN I'LL HAVE TO.'

'That's a bit selfish.'

'THERE'S NO POINT IN ARGUING BECAUSE I ALREADY KNOW YOU'RE GOING TO DO IT.'

'Stop being annoying.'

'NO YOU DON'T.'

They both looked at the screen, mystified.

'We can't do anything dressed like this,' said Trafalgar, 'We've got to go home to change.'

'OH YES THERE IS.'

'There aren't any other jobs anyway,' Trafalgar went on. 'We've done them all.'

Stilts whispered in his ear. 'It's got it wrong. It's answering the *next* thing you say. It should have said

''NO YOU DON'T'' *after* you said we had to go home to change.'

'STOP WHISPERING,' said the screen. 'I KNOW I GET IT WRONG ROUND ABOUT HERE. IT'S VERY HARD TRYING TO REMEMBER EVERYTHING IN THE RIGHT ORDER. JUST THINK ABOUT IT. THERE'S DEFINITELY SOMETHING YOU'VE FOR-GOTTEN TO SORT OUT.'

Stilts looked through the jobs list on the screen. They were all ticked off. As he looked there was a momentary smell of hot plastic and a wisp of smoke. A new job appeared on the screen.

'JOB 16,' it said. 'Sort out O'Barron muddle.'

'Oh really,' he said, 'I don't think that's at all fair. We've done all the rest.'

Trafalgar looked over his shoulder. 'I know, but it's right, isn't it? If we don't do something, there's going to be hell to pay when we get back.'

'You're always on his side.'

'I suppose I'm bound to be, really.'

'All right then, if you're so smart. What do you sug-gest we do?'

'I think we've just got to make a clean breast of it. We'll go and pick up O'Barron and take him back to Lemmon's enquiry and when we get there, we'll just have to explain what really happened. That's the only decent, honest way.'

They both contemplated the thought in silence for a while.

'No, we can't do that,' they both said at once.

Sir J.E.E. Dalberg Acton (1834–1902) hit the nail on the head when he said, 'Power tends to corrupt and absolute power corrupts absolutely.'

By the time the remnants of this saying reached the

year 95 SEGS, the mice had modified it somewhat so that the saying Trafalgar and Stilts knew was 'power tends to cost money and absolute power costs absolutely masses.' This failed to give the same powerful moral warning as the original version but they were at least vaguely familiar with the concept.

Bluto O'Barron had been completely corrupted by power. When they first knew him as Minister of Knowledge before that job passed to Genghis Lemmon, he had been a vain, unpleasant, big-headed, cowardly man.

Then he dropped the 'Mr Nice Guy' act.

During the voyage of the TS *Titanic* he had sensed what it was like to be an absolute dictator when he finally came to the conclusion that he was the real King Elvis, wearer of the Blue Suede Crown. In the end even that hadn't seemed quite enough so he declared himself Emperor of the World. He was by this time in a fairly unstable mental condition having been forced to spend many years towing large blocks of stone up earth ramps with only a flock of sheep for his motive power and the world of which he had declared himself Emperor had nobody else left awake in it except for the rest of the crew of the *Titanic*. For all that, they hadn't planned to strand him there, however richly he may have deserved what happened. It was, in fact, entirely his own fault that that was the result.

Trafalgar and Stilts knew exactly where and when they'd left him. He'd been wearing the tattered remnants of a long wedding dress from his interrupted attempt at forcing Anya to marry him. They'd last seen him singing 'Lonesome Tonight' extremely badly in the middle of Grand Central Fortress, New York, as the *Titanic* had whisked them off for its final and rather terminal rendezvous with a collapsing building. It was the work of a moment, using the time machine's map and its log of previous journeys, to set their destination for the same place a minute or two later. It was the work of rather more moments to persuade themselves that they had no choice but to press the button.

Everything went dark and there was a horrible off-key howling noise from outside the door.

'Good heavens,' said Trafalgar, horrified. 'What's THAT?'

'Verse four, I think,' said Stilts. 'At least he's still here.'

They opened the door and looked out at the only other occupant of the entire world.

In the thirty or forty seconds which had elapsed since they had last been there several months earlier, Bluto O'Barron had managed to remain a truly repulsive sight. His multicoloured wedding dress was made out of the remains of the *Titanic*'s signal flags and the veil now hung crookedly over one ear. His eyes were staring wildly and what he was doing with his pelvis looked more like a man being attacked by flesh-eating Y-fronts than anything inspired by the King of rock and roll.

The arrival of the flattened rock seemed to come as no surprise. He barely glanced at it, or at Trafalgar and Stilts as they emerged from it. He was singing a song and nothing was going to stop him. They looked around them at the dismantling of the full-sized world. A small yellow machine was eating its way through the wall next to them and beyond it they could see the blackened remnants of New York. The final years of famine and violence had been hard on the city. The buildings were blackened and twisted and the potholed streets were running with stinking filth.

'Funny, isn't it?' said Stilts. 'Just think. All those people down there in the cellars, snoring away in the sleep pods, all getting smaller, cell by cell, until in five hundred years' time they'll . . .'

'Silence!' roared a voice behind them and they turned to see that O'Barron had finished his song and was advancing towards them with a look of fury on his face.

'Who dares interrupt the Emperor?' he bawled.

'It's Cheesemaker and Hurlock,' Stilts explained, with what Trafalgar thought was far more politeness than the situation demanded. 'We've come to give you a lift back.'

'There are no people now!' roared O'Barron. 'I am the King of the Sheep therefore you are sheep. I name you Ewe and Ewe.'

'Well that's not very clever,' said Trafalgar crossly. 'Can't you do better than that?'

'Silence, Ewe.'

'Get in the rock, for heaven's sake.'

'You dare give me orders? Me, the Emperor?'

'Yes.'

'You'll have to catch me first,' said O'Barron and ran out through the hole in the wall.

'Shall we just not bother?' said Stilts. 'I'd forgotten just how much I loathe him.'

'We'll have to go after him,' said Trafalgar resignedly. 'It's the only way.'

It was, in some ways, quite an interesting hour they spent running through the remains of the city following O'Barron as he raced through the streets. Everywhere the little yellow machines were munching away at the gaunt, gigantic buildings, separating the materials and spewing them into the hoppers from which, during the next five hundred years, the new miniature world would be rebuilt. O'Barron was surprisingly fast on his feet, probably due to the years of hard manual labour in Olvisland and they just couldn't overtake him. They'd catch glimpses of him disappearing around the next corner but that was as near as they could get.

'He's going in a big circle,' Stilts panted.

'That's right, I think he's heading back to the Fortress.'

They stopped and looked at each other and the same thought dawned on both of them like milk going sour.

'The rock!'

Fear lent wings to their feet and charged them interest in sweat as they hurtled after O'Barron and into the Fortress. They jumped through the hole in the wall which led back into the central hall and saw the rock. Its door was just closing.

'Whoops,' said Trafalgar.

'You're a master of understatement, really, aren't you?' said Stilts. 'I mean to say "whoops" hardly covers it, does it? Here we are, two of the only three beings still at large on the surface of a dead planet populated entirely by robot demolition crews. The only other living being, who happens to be completely demented, is currently at the controls of our only means of escape and the best you can manage is "whoops".'

'You don't think he knows how to work it, do you?'

'Of course he does. He's watched me do it enough times.'

'Oh. Well maybe I'll upgrade "whoops" to "blimey".'

'Why are you taking it so calmly?'

'The usual reason. I know I get out of it because I've still got to do the . . .' Trafalgar's voice trailed off.

'. . . the rest of the jobs?'

'Er, yes.'

'You mean the jobs you've finished doing now.'

'That's the ones. Oh bugger.'

'I think that's still an understatement.'

212

They both looked at the rock, wondering what O'Barron was up to inside it. Then they panicked.

'Quick,' yelled Stilts, 'let's get on top of it.'

Before they could move, the rock disappeared.

Inside the rock, O'Barron had tried ordering the machine to take him to his royal palace in the Kingdom of Graceland but it ignored him. This was because he did it by shouting and the computer wasn't designed for voice input. He then told it he was placing it under arrest for treason and insubordination and it still ignored him.

Then he started hitting it.

Stilts was right when he said that O'Barron had watched him using the controls many times but, by O'Barron's personal calendar, that had been many years earlier and they'd been tough years at that. He no longer had the slightest idea of how to work the controls of the machine. That, unfortunately, didn't stop him aiming his fists at the keyboard.

The first keys he hit with his right fist made the machine jump forward two minutes. The next blow with his left fist made it jump back a minute. The third blow put it forward by the same minute. Confused by the mind-bending effects of time travel, he kept hammering away at these keys one after the other until he got bored.

This had an interesting effect.

One minute passed in which neither Trafalgar nor Stilts really started to come to terms with the idea that they were stranded alone on a planet with no food, no company and no chance of rescue. At the start of the next minute, eighty-four rocks reappeared because O'Barron had pressed both buttons a total of eighty-four times. Because of the solid object proximity avoidance

213

device, the rocks avoided major disasters but the great hall which had been so completely empty of rocks for that first nerveracking minute was suddenly completely full of rocks stacked side by side and tilted on top of each other.

They wasted most of the next minute gaping at the rock pile then Trafalgar yelled, 'Quick, come on!'

He clambered on to the nearest rock and turned to see Stilts standing there irresolute.

'How do you know it's the right one?' said Stilts.

Through the crashing pain of the most extreme headache in the history of headaches, Trafalgar gestured around. Every rock now had a Trafalgar on it.

'It doesn't matter,' he said through gritted teeth. 'Just get on.'

Stilts jumped at the rock a second too late. Abruptly all the rocks and all the Trafalgars blinked out, leaving him in a smoke-filled hall, all by himself.

SEVENTEEN

When O'Barron had finally had enough of pounding the keyboard with his fists, he had given it a final indignant sideways flick, riffling his fingers across the keys like a psychotic jazz pianist with a bad grudge against his piano. This brought up the 'Next Destination' screen. Destiny has an inevitability about it which can sometimes be quite irritating. In this case Stilts had already started to programme the screen with the coordinates for their return home. He'd only got as far as copying off the data from the map on the screen for their departure point and, not wanting to collide with themselves, he had added an hour or two for their arrival back. When O'Barron played his final riff, the machine obediently jumped to almost exactly where it was told.

It is not a criticism of the manufacturing standards of time machines to say that it was no longer in perfect working order. No one had ever built it with the idea in mind that it should have to serve as part of the foundations for the Leaning Tower of Pisa, although it is true that there had been no *specific* warning in the instruction manual against such use. Its horizontal spacial calibration was slightly out, but only by fifteen or twenty feet. It ended up not on the edge of the rubble pile from where it had left, but somewhere in the middle.

This was moderately inconvenient for O'Barron, who was inside it, and extremely inconvenient for Trafalgar, who had been kneeling on top of it. O'Barron suddenly found himself still inside the rock but now in total darkness and buried under twenty feet of rubble. Trafalgar would have equally suddenly found himself outside the rock in total darkness buried under twenty feet of rubble if he had still been in a state to find himself anywhere. While nobody would have voluntarily chosen either of those two positions, it is probable that, if forced, most would have gone for the O'Barron option.

Both their lives were saved by the time machine's built-in safeguards in the form of the solid object proximity avoidance device which meant that the machine tried its very best to rematerialise both itself and its cargo into suitably empty space. There wasn't enough empty space available inside the mound, but it did everything it could. It squeezed Trafalgar into a narrow gap between two large lumps of concrete and then caused a minor earthquake inside the mound by inserting the battered rock into a space half its size between several giant lumps of rubble.

From the outside, the effect was spectacular and as it happened, there was an audience on the spot to appreciate it. Lemmon's enquiry had just reconvened as the rock arrived back. The Minister sat down at his table, pounded on it with his gavel and glared around at his audience which consisted once more of the rest of the former crew of the *Titanic* plus a doubled contingent of security guards from the Death Watch.

'Order, order,' said Lemmon.

The smallest member of the Death Watch had been daydreaming.

'Pie, chips and beans, please,' he said.

'Silence!' roared the Sergeant in his outdoor voice. 'The Minister orders first, you 'orrible young man. What would you like to order, Minister?'

Lemmon winced and looked puzzled. 'I meant everybody should be quiet, Sergeant.'

'Everybody is being quiet, SAH!'

'Everybody except you, Sergeant.'

'That's because I'm telling you that everybody is being quiet, SAH!'

'Fine, Sergeant. You've told me now.'

'Yes, SAH!'

Lemmon looked nervously at the Sergeant. 'Right then,' he said. 'This enquiry is hereby convened for the purpose of discovering the truth concerning the disappearance of former Minister, Bluto O'Barron. Are we all present?'

The *Titanic*'s crew looked at each other and shuffled their feet.

'I see we're not,' said Lemmon. 'Where are Trafalgar Hurlock and Stilton Cheesemaker?'

Feet went on shuffling.

'We don't know, sir,' said Puckeridge. 'We haven't seen them since this morning.'

'A sign of guilt perhaps?' suggested Lemmon. 'Does anyone here have any explanation for their absence?'

There was a long silence broken only by a small throat-clearing noise from the smallest member of the Death Watch.

'Yes?' said Lemmon encouragingly, turning to look at him.

'Er . . .'

'Soldier!' bawled the Sergeant. 'Don't speak hunless you are haddressed.'

'I *did* haddress . . . I mean address him, Sergeant,' said Lemmon.

'Soldier!' bawled the Sergeant. 'Don't not speak when you are being haddressed. That is a *horder!*'

'Um . . . It's just . . .'

'Yes?' said Lemmon encouragingly.

'Perhaps they were spirited away, sir.'

'Nonsense,' said Lemmon testily.

'But, sir. The Gulliver, *he* was spirited away, sir – right before our eyes, sir, and my aunt Bernard, she says the mound is haunted and . . .'

'Soldier,' said Lemmon sternly. 'I am quite sure we will discover there is a perfectly rational explanation for whatever may have happened to the Gulliver earlier today and I firmly believe that as far as the absence of Hurlock and Cheesemaker goes, we do not need to concern ourselves with supernatural events in any . . .'

This was the exact moment at which the rock chose to rematerialise inside the mound. From the outside the event was extremely unusual. The entire mound suddenly shook with a rumbling, rending sound. Clouds of dust spurted out through every tiny hole and a long subsiding groan echoed from deep down below. A strange noise could be heard almost as if a voice was shouting far underground. The entire Death Watch took to their heels and, if Lemmon hadn't got tangled up in his table, it looked likely that he would have followed. The crew of the *Titanic*, who had become more used to events like this, sniffed appreciatively. They could smell the giveaway smoke of a time jump and they watched closely to see what would happen next, particularly Anya who had a peculiar and unexpected smile on her beautiful face.

'Come back here!' Lemmon bawled at his retreating guard. It took a few minutes for the Sergeant to round them up, then, white-faced and nervous, they slow-marched back on tip-toe to re-take their places.

'Exercises, SAH!' explained the Sergeant unconvincingly. 'Just practising their strategic outflanking manoeuvres, SAH!'

'As I was saying,' said Lemmon, squashingly, 'there is no supernatural dimension to this affair. What you just heard was some sort of subsidence underground – a complete coincidence, I am quite sure.' He glared challengingly at the crew of the *Titanic*. 'Now, let's see. I am going to put you all under oath to tell the truth. You first.'

He pointed to Sopwith Camel who shambled forward and repeated the words of the oath on the card in front of him, then looked expectantly at Lemmon.

'I want to know exactly when was the last time you saw Minister O'Barron,' said Lemmon.

Sopwith thought hard. 'Excuse me, Minister,' he said, 'but do you mean by that the most recent date?'

'Of course I do,' said Lemmon which was an understandable mistake for one who had not actually taken part in any form of time travel himself.

'Here,' said Sopwith, cheerfully, 'at the launch of the *Titanic*.'

Lemmon was no fool, however, and when he took note of the expression of relief on Sopwith's face, he thought hard.

'Aha!' he said. 'Let me rephrase that. What, with reference to the passing of time *solely in the order as perceived by you*, was the final occasion on which you saw Minister O'Barron?'

Sopwith hesitated over this for several seconds while Lemmon watched him like a hawk then he looked up and his expression changed to one of shock. He pointed a quivering finger past Lemmon to the mound.

'Right now,' he said with difficulty. 'Look behind you.'

The dead silence that followed as Lemmon slowly pivoted round was shattered by the pounding of twenty pairs of army boots as the Death Watch took to their heels once more.

* * *

Inside the rock, O'Barron had recovered from the shock of the violent landing and shouted at the door to open itself several times before reluctantly putting his shoulder to it himself. It creaked open just far enough to let him out into a dark and narrow gap between lumps of rubble. There was a tiny gleam of daylight far ahead.

'At last,' he shouted. 'My true kingdom awaits. I have passed through great ordeals in the magical realms of dangerous enchantment down in the deepest dungeons of the netherworld from which I must now ascend to claim my rightful throne. All else was mere preparation for this most glorious moment of destiny!' He looked at the broken masonry blocking the way and began to worm his way upwards.

Minister Lemmon tried very hard to be calm and rational and failed utterly. The figure which had just crawled from the mound was a truly terrifying sight. O'Barron's wedding dress was now ripped, torn and filthy. O'Barron himself had aged several years since Lemmon had last seen him, but Lemmon knew who it was at once.

He leapt straight to the wrong conclusion. The last fleeting remnants of rational calmness suggested to him that the upheaval inside the mound must be linked to the reappearance of O'Barron. The most likely theory was that O'Barron must have been trapped inside the remains of the *Titanic* for all the intervening months until some subterranean collapse had freed him. That would account for his wild, gaunt appearance. What on earth could he have found to eat and drink down there? Insects and rainwater? Rational calmness gave up trying to suggest anything to him and it fled in the same direction as the Death Watch.

'Minister,' he gasped. 'I mean ex-Minister, you're alive.'

'Kneel!' bellowed O'Barron.

'Er, no, it's Genghis actually.'

'Down on your knees, or die! No one stands in the presence of the Emperor of the Universe and King of the Golden Discs.'

'Um, no, I don't expect they do. Where is he?' Lemmon looked warily at the mound as if someone else was likely to emerge.

'IT IS I! Summon my slaves or I shall have you beheaded.'

'Slaves, right. Um, let me see, slaves.'

The crew of the *Titanic* were standing there, stunned by O'Barron's reappearance, wondering how long it would take before he blew the gaff. They recognised the wedding dress only too well. Lemmon looked at them.

'Will these do for slaves?' he said.

'THESE?' yelled O'Barron in fury. 'These are the rebellious and disobedient horde who abandoned me in the middle of the stones for years on end, with only the sheep as my subjects. Get me some real slaves, fool, and if you do it quickly I shall spare your miserable life and you shall tread out the measure of your pitiful days in the glorious satisfaction of serving me.'

'Years?' said Lemmon feebly. 'Abandoned for years? But you've only been in there for a few months.'

'HOW DARE YOU ARGUE WITH ME,' thundered O'Barron advancing on him menacingly.

'Go and get some help,' Lemmon hissed to Sopwith Camel out of the corner of his mouth. 'The sort of help that comes with sedatives, nets and a padded van.'

Sopwith shot off as fast as his legs could carry his rather unfairly-sized body.

Trafalgar had survived the rock's chaotic arrival in the rubble pile perfectly intact as it had fitted him neatly, though extremely tightly, in between the lumps of masonry. It was what happened immediately afterwards that hurt. The upheaval in the pile sent concrete and brick flying in all directions and one of the bricks, ricocheting down through the gaps, hit him hard on the head. Everything went even blacker than it already was. When he came round a few minutes later with an extremely sore head, it was hard to tell which were spots in front of his eyes and which were gleams of daylight pointing to the way out. It took him several minutes of intense and painful effort to claw a way through the rubble towards the world outside. When he got within a foot or two of freedom he paused to catch his breath, and found he could see through the narrow gap some extraordinary things going on outside. O'Barron was fighting a rearguard action against at least a dozen Emergency Squad paramedics who were trying to put him in an ambulance. As he watched, they gave a final heave, tipped him and half their number inside and slammed the door shut. The ambulance went off, swaying from side to side to a chorus of thuds and grunts from within.

Lemmon walked back to sit at his table, only a few feet from where Trafalgar was lying looking out.

'Right,' he heard Lemmon say in a voice that had a definite tremble in it. 'I call this meeting to order one last time. The release of ex-Minister O'Barron clearly changes things, but there are still matters we need to get to the bottom of.'

He stopped there. Genghis Lemmon was essentially a sensible person but sense didn't go very well with recent events and he could no longer remember what it was he was trying to get to the bottom of. 'If nothing else,' he continued with a trace of desperation, 'where *are* Hurlock and Cheesemaker?'

That was too much for Trafalgar. He knew perfectly well where *he* was but Stilts? Stilts was lost back in the echoing past, nearly six hundred years earlier. A choking sob rose in his throat.

'Dead,' he moaned. 'Dead, dead. He's deeeeeaaaaad, ooooooh.'

He hadn't meant it to be quite so loud.

There was a sudden silence outside. Every eye had turned to the mound. He levered himself awkwardly out, groaning with the pain from the bump on his head, and before he could say anything, everyone but Anya had run away.

From their point of view it was not really a surprising reaction. Trafalgar had completely forgotten that he was still dressed in the long white robes from his brief career as a statue and that his face was covered in white paint, now liberally smeared with dust and dirt from his escape through the rubble pile. Even Lemmon, his nerves already on edge from O'Barron's return, found it too much to take when a wailing, ghostly figure suddenly rose into view from the solid earth. The Minister turned and ran and the crew of the *Titanic* decided to follow.

All except Anya.

She handed Trafalgar a small suitcase, blew him a kiss and walked off smiling, leaving him standing there with his mouth opening and closing wordlessly.

The suitcase contained some well-chosen items. A set of clothes he had never seen before but which suited him rather well, a large box of face-wipes which helped get most of the paint off, and a towel. In ten minutes, he was back in better physical shape and if he could have stopped brooding about what had happened to Stilts, he might have been only as unhappy as he always was when thinking about Anya. But when he put on the overalls he felt the hard edges of an envelope in the pocket. The note inside was carefully printed out. It gave a list of coordinates. 'Useful advice from one who knows you well,' it said. 'Go back to your wedding night. Tell Anya to leave the other man alone.'

It made him realise that somewhere in the mound was the time machine, that O'Barron had clearly found a way out of the wreckage to get to the surface, and that therefore if he could only get back down to it the same way, he might well be able to obey the note. On the other hand if he could do that, he might also be able to go back and rescue Stilts. Excited and suddenly hopeful, he began to explore the mound and quickly found the fresh hole from which O'Barron must have escaped. He was down the hole, headfirst, in a flash and after squirming his way painfully through its twists and turns, he arrived at what was left of the rock and squirmed through the partly-open door.

There was even less space inside than there had been before. The roof had been ripped half off and a large lump of concrete had come through, landing on the control desk, missing the time machine and the monitor screen. The keyboard was mostly untouched.

Mostly wasn't quite good enough.

Three-quarters of it was still there. The problem lay with the other quarter, which had been smashed into tiny fragments of plastic. This included quite a large chunk of the top row of keys.

Trafalgar, peering at the remains in the gloom, switched on the machine without much hope but the screen came to life just as it should. In the past he had usually left the controls to Stilts, but he felt he knew enough to have a go. The map screen gave him the coordinates of the spot where he'd last seen Stilts plus the date and the time. The date was 1/1/2112 and the time was 14.33. He had no problem entering the date in. It was the time that proved difficult. The key with '4' on it had disappeared completely. In the end, he settled on 15.00 as the nearest he could get. Surely Stilts couldn't get into too much trouble in half an hour, he thought.

Optimism is a wonderful thing.

As time jumps go this one was both more dramatic and less comfortable than most. The damage to the rock was so severe that in trying to separate itself from the rubble pile it also managed to separate itself from itself. In the usual confusing horror of time travel, at that instant when the air seemed to turn to iridescent blue treacle and the time traveller felt his body being folded along a number of extremely painful dotted lines, Trafalgar also felt himself falling through what had recently been the floor. He was left clinging by his fingertips to the jagged edge of something he couldn't see, wondering what would happen to him if he let go. He didn't find out, which was just as well because it almost certainly wouldn't have been very nice. Instead, he and the remains of the rock landed on the familiar floor of Grand Central Fortress. It would have been quite a funny sight if there had been anybody looking but there wasn't.

Stilts was nowhere to be seen.

Trafalgar inspected his means of transport morosely. The rock was now half a rock. It looked as if someone had turned it into a cutaway model of a time vehicle. Wherever it came from, he just hoped nobody was ever going to ask for it back. He looked around at the empty hall then walked out of the Fortress to the disappearing streets of old New York where the only moving things were the recycling robots.

'Stilts!' he roared at the top of his voice and listened

for a reply. There was none. He walked a hundred yards and tried again but the effect was the same. In the next three hours, he went in widening circles around the Fortress, shouting until his voice was hoarse, then, in despair, he gave up and went back to where he started. The great hall was even emptier than it had been before.

Half a rock would have been better than no rock but there wasn't even that. The time vehicle had vanished.

EIGHTEEN

A robot was busy dismantling the Fortress's outside wall, prising the blocks apart and putting them in the hopper on its back. Trafalgar gazed at it, dully. Then he noticed the writing. On the wall were two lines of a message written in orange paint in Stilts's writing. They both ended at the jagged hole where the robot was taking the wall to pieces, then started again several feet further on at the other side of the hole. The words in the middle of both sentences had already been dismantled.

The top line said, 'Trafalgar, if you've come back. I've had a brilliant idea. I'm . . . Time's Square.'

The second line immediately below it said, 'The robot's put the time machine in . . . Good luck.'

'Oh, well done,' said Trafalgar sarcastically to the robot, but sarcasm rather loses its force when there's only an inanimate object with no ears on the receiving end of it.

The robot, its hopper full up, trundled off to unload in the huge recycling bin outside. Trafalgar, seized by the desperate idea that he might manage to find all the bits of the wall with the missing letters, ran after it and tried to climb the side of the bin to look in. It was too high. There was a hissing noise and he saw that the robot's hopper was starting to rise on hydraulic rams so he leapt after it and clung to the side as it went up and up then tilted to disgorge its contents into the bin. That swung him against the outside of the bin and he managed to grab the edge of it, dangling from the outside as the hopper tipped up. He heard the contents of the hopper clattering down on to something inside the bin that clanged, boinged and crunched under the hail of building materials. Pulling himself up, he managed to get his head over the rim of the bin and looked down into it.

He'd found the rock.

The robot had decided to recycle it while he'd been away and it was now tilted at a crazy angle, open side uppermost, half buried under a mound of mixed rubble. Another hopperful would have completely covered it. Trafalgar hauled himself up over the edge and fell heavily into the bin as the robot retracted its hopper, then, working frantically, he began to scoop enough of the rubble out of the way to unearth the control desk. He got it free, but there was now a crack right across the monitor screen and more of the keyboard had fallen off. A shadow loomed over him, and he looked up. Another robot hopper swayed over him. He pressed the 'on' button and, against all odds, the cracked monitor came to life with a fainter and more discordant version of its usual greeting. Just as the first bricks began to hurtle down towards him, he pressed 'Last Destination' and hoped for the best. Even being inside the *Titanic*'s mound would be better than this.

Time travel with added builders' rubble was something he could easily learn to live without. In the brief period of pain when he was between times, gravity and most of the laws of physics ceased to have much hold. Some of the smaller bits of rubble got up his nose, while others were flung off into back eddies of the space-time continuum, creating minor chaos wherever they landed. One small cube of reinforced concrete kept twentieth-century archaeologists occupied for years by turning up inside a Minoan wine jar they had just excavated from an ancient Greek palace. Another hit King Harold on the helmet just as he was feeling moderately optimistic about kicking the Normans back into the sea. He looked up to see what it was just in time to get a momentary close-up view of the sharp end of an arrow and all he got out of the experience was a reputation as a loser and a small place on a large tapestry.

These things happen when you time travel without securing your load properly first.

Trafalgar was spared having to dig himself out of the *Titanic*'s mound yet again by the increasingly unreliable state of the time machine which returned to exactly the right time but exactly the wrong place, balancing for a fraction of a second on the very top of the mound still at the same crazy angle before tipping over and cartwheeling down it like a catherine wheel, hurling Trafalgar and his pile of rubble out on to the ground before coming to rest upside down in the middle of the road. He sat on the ground surrounded by bits of bricks and giant pre-Sleep-era concrete blocks with orange lettering on them. The nearest one said 'eep'. The next one to it said 'recycl'. There was an 'ing' that matched it, an 'ake me', an 'ement' and the rest was a whole lot of separate letters.

There was little likelihood of being disturbed. The recent chain of apparently supernatural events at the mound would probably make sure nobody came near it for weeks, so he spent an hour on his hands and knees trying to arrange the letters in such a way that they made sense. The best he could get was 'take me recycling cement walruses' which didn't advance the sum of human knowledge by any significant amount.

What was he trying to tell me, he kept asking himself. Time's square indeed. It was one of those expressions you never really thought about, like 'When in Bognor, do what the Romans do.' Did it have some crucial meaning that might help him save Stilts if he could only crack it? He thought hard. If only he could get the right angle on it. Right angle? Four right angles made a square. Time's square. The way ahead always lies round a blind corner. Go round enough blind corners and you can creep up on yourself from behind. That sounded like a pretty good definition of time travel as he'd experienced it so far, but it didn't really help.

All at once, Trafalgar decided he'd had enough. Time travel had never been his idea in the first place and so far it had caused him nothing but trouble. It had lost him his girl and his best friend and he wasn't going to take any more. In a new mood of determination, he looked again at the note in the envelope and knew it was time to sort things out.

What was left of the rock was now little more than a bent sheet of metal with the control desk hanging off it, housing a cracked and dusty monitor, the time machine itself and the remains of the keyboard. The coordinates written on the note didn't include any of the missing numbers, which was just as well, so he fed them in, hanging on to the desk like a rodeo rider waiting for his tortoise to start bucking, and pressed the button with a grim and defiant glare on his face.

The rock splash-landed in deep mud, which covered Trafalgar from head to foot. It was a dark night and Trafalgar, eyes full of the foul stuff, couldn't see a thing but he heard a startled gasp from nearby. Two people were walking away rather nervously. It was an oddly familiar scene and with a new certainty in his heart, he began to follow. They went out of sight round the next corner, looking anxiously back behind them, and he stopped at the corner to take a cautious peek round it.

The 'Rubber Chicken' restaurant was brightly lit and the strains of gypsy music sounded from inside, growing suddenly louder as the door opened and the couple went in. He saw them at a table in the window and the gypsy trio surrounded them immediately, their bows scraping away at the strings of their trombones. Trafalgar walked round to the back of the restaurant where he found a hose pipe and washed himself down to clean off the mud, then he stepped in through the back door, dripping wet, cold and furious.

His timing was perfect. Anya came through the door ahead of him, looking from side to side. Then she noticed him, gasped and stood stock still, staring at him.

'How did you . . .' she began.

'Anya,' he snarled, 'you keep quiet and listen to me, OK? I'm not in a mood to argue about this. You've got to leave this other guy alone.'

'What other . . .'

'It's *me* you married, not him, whoever he is. I don't know where you're planning to go right now but you just change your mind, understood?'

'But . . .'

'But nothing. Leaving by the back door, were you?'

'No, I . . .'

'Don't try to deny it. I've been here before, you see. I know what happens. I know you go out of the back door and that's the last he sees of you.'

'The last *who* sees of me?'

'HIM! In there!' Trafalgar pointed towards the restaurant. 'You get back in there.'

'But I only came out to go to the loo,' Anya said weakly. 'Hang on a minute. I'll be right back.'

Trafalgar stood guard over the lavatory door to make sure, hoping there wasn't a window she could climb out of. It was only then that he began to think clearly and doubts started to grow in his mind.

She couldn't go back in to the restaurant because she hadn't. She had to go off with someone else because she did. This was completely pointless because this section of time had already been done once and as he knew all too well, it couldn't be re-done.

The door opened. Anya stood there, smiling nervously at him.

'I'm so glad,' she said, 'so very, very glad. You can *talk* to me. This is the man I married. This is the man who punched O'Barron on the jaw. This is the brave, bold decisive Trafalgar I love.' She stared at his face. 'You even look different somehow. You look harder, tougher.'

'Wetter,' he added, looking back at the restaurant with regret, knowing how much Trafalgar 1 would inevitably be suffering in there in a few minutes' time, then he turned back to Anya, took her arm and the man who had finally become Trafalgar 2 led his bride out of the back door.

That, of course, wasn't by any means the end of it. It took a long time for him to tell Anya the whole complicated story and there were lots of other things they wanted to do as well as talk, but perfect happiness was spoilt by two things. The minor irritation was that Trafalgar was now more or less confined to Anya's flat while she went out to work. The danger of causing some major time paradox was simply too great with his earlier self living only a block or two away. It didn't really help that he already knew they hadn't bumped into each other during that period. The chance still remained that something else *had* happened which he simply hadn't yet found out about.

That paled into insignificance compared to the painful knowledge that the earlier version of Stilts was now somewhere nearby, not knowing that he was going to end his days five hundred and ninety-five years earlier in a deserted city all because Trafalgar had come back too late to rescue him. Trafalgar spent hours trying to get the time machine back into working order. He fitted a new keyboard but whatever he tried, he could no longer get it to come to life at all. Stilts would have managed it easily, he knew all too well, but he lacked Stilts's technical skill.

'Anya,' he said one night, 'we could go and find Stilts, *this* Stilts I mean, and ask him to fix it for us, couldn't we?'

She looked doubtful. 'But then he'd know you'd done that and you'd know.'

'Not if we told him it was terribly important that he kept it a secret. We could even decide in advance what the rest of the message on the wall was going to say.'

She still looked doubtful. 'He's not like that, is he? He's a terrible actor. I'm sure you would already know that's what had happened. He could never keep it to himself.'

'No, you're right. Oh dear.'

Then Anya had her big idea. 'There's John,' she said.

'How do you mean?'

'He hasn't been found yet, has he? He's still in a sleep pod down in the Ministry basement.'

'That's right.'

'Supposing we give him a message.'

'How will that help?'

'Well, think about it. You told me he borrowed the time machine for a while in Italy.'

'That's right.'

'And it was in good working order then?'

'Yes.'

'If you asked him to, surely he'd go and rescue Stilts

233

for you. You could give him the right coordinates so that he got to Grand Central Fortress and rescued Stilts just before you arrived back there. That would explain why Stilts wasn't there.'

Trafalgar brightened. 'That's brilliant,' he said. 'We could ask him to drop Stilts off again any time we liked from now on. You're *so* clever.'

'That's it. After all it's still a little while until they first discover John and this whole thing starts happening. He could bring him back in a week or two, couldn't he?'

'You're wonderful,' said Trafalgar and the next few minutes were unbearably sloppy.

Anya still worked at the Ministry of Knowledge some of the time and it proved very easy for her to stay on late the next day when everybody else had gone home and let Trafalgar, shrouded in a cloak, in through the back door. They made their way down the stairs to the basement and then down the next stairs to the sub-basement and finally down the final stairs to the extremely dusty sub-sub-basement where the sleep pods lay undiscovered. They looked at the one containing John. They'd written him a polite letter explaining exactly what he needed to do when the time came.

'Where are we going to leave it?' said Trafalgar.

'Propped up on the outside?'

'But then they'll see it when they find him.'

'Inside then?'

'How do we do that without opening up the pod?'

'You're right, we can't. We'll just have to open the pod, put it in his pocket and hope he finds it.'

'I don't think this is going to work,' said Trafalgar gloomily. 'How do we open the pod without waking him up?'

'There must be a way. Let's have a look at the other

pods to see how *they* work. They're empty, aren't they?'

'That's right. They take the empty ones upstairs later, don't they? When it gets to it, I mean. It was only this last one that was full.'

Anya walked across to one of the other pods and wiped the instruction plate clean with her sleeve.

'It says, "To open in emergency, press blue button. Allow ten minutes for resuscitation procedure to take place."'

'You'd better press it. If we have a look at the mechanism we might find some way that we can put a letter in the other one.'

Nothing happened straightaway. After a while there was a whining noise and a small jet of steam began to squirt out of a nozzle in the side of the pod. Under the dust, bright letters spelt out a mostly-hidden message.

'I remember what that says,' Trafalgar said confidently. 'Stand clear, pod opening. Hold your noses.'

'Why do you have to hold your noses?' asked Anya, interested.

'Well you see, normally in a full pod, there's quite a lot of horrible body odours that build up over five hundred and ninety-five years but this one's empty so it won't sme . . . phworrr, euuggggh, yeeuuuck.'

'It won't what did you . . . yeeech, wugger, bleeeuuch.'

She beat Trafalgar to the exit door by a clear yard and they stopped, chests heaving, sucking in relatively fresh air.

'Interesting,' said Trafalgar. 'Another theory bites the dust. It must be some chemical smell from the plastic they're made out of, I suppose.'

'No, no,' said a voice from the pod. 'That's not it at all.'

It was a voice they both knew, even if it did sound a bit choked up with a very, very long sleep.

'Stilts!' they yelled in united delight.

'Hello,' he said amiably, sitting up in the pod and blinking. 'You got my message then.'

'It was simple really,' he explained when they'd done their best to cover their tracks in the dust and got him back to Anya's for a good wash and some fresh clothes. 'I waited a few minutes after you'd gone expecting you to come back and when you didn't I knew I was in trouble. Then I just had this brilliant idea. I mean, I knew roughly where the sleep pods were found and it didn't take me long to locate the one John had put himself in. There were two more there and I knew they were empty by the time John woke up. I set the controls to wake up about now then I found the paint and told you where to come and find me if you did manage to come back. Good, eh?'

'Good! Good, you say!' said Trafalgar. 'The message got dismantled. I was at my wits' end. What was all that rubbish about time's square?'

'No, no,' said Stilts. 'That's capital T capital S. Time's Square. That's where the pods were, under Time's Square. It was a place in those days. It wasn't far away at all.' He shrugged. 'Oh well,' he said philosophically, 'all's well that ends smaller.'

'You were taking a risk,' Anya said. 'It might have shrunk you all over again. You could have come out tiny.'

'No chance,' he said. 'There's a switch you turn off, that's all. I knew John had managed it, so I had a good look. Now, I guess we can just get back to normal life again.'

'Not really, no,' said Trafalgar, 'at least not for a few weeks.'

'Why not?'

'Because there's another one of you around this town *and* another one of me and it wouldn't do to get in any mix-ups.'

'Oh, no. You woke me up too early.'

'Come off it. You're hardly short of sleep.'

'I'd programmed it just right. What do we do now?'

'You'll both have to stay at my place, that's all,' said Anya. 'We'll manage somehow.'

That night, they carried what was left of the working parts of the rock into Anya's apartment and Stilts started work to see if there was anything at all he could do. He worked on it all the next day too and time passed quite quickly for the first couple of hours, then quite slowly for the next two and then crawled along.

'I'll go mad stuck in here for much longer,' said Stilts, putting down his soldering iron morosely. 'I need some fresh air.'

'Is that thing going to work?'

'I don't think so. The only bit I can get any life out of at all is the fast forward.'

They looked at each other. 'That's not such a bad idea,' said Trafalgar. 'At least we could go out for a walk. Nobody would see us.'

They put on a wrist-band each. Stilts set the machine carefully and pressed the button. Outside the window, everything turned red as life seemed to stop in its tracks. People in the street slowed from walking pace to something like the speed of an hour hand on an old clock. A bird hung in midair in the deep silence.

'Let's go,' said Stilts. 'Be careful what you touch. We don't want any fires.'

They walked down towards the 'Rubber Chicken' restaurant as Trafalgar explained everything that had happened last time he'd been there, weaving their way in between the people on the pavements. Their route took them past the Gravesend Geriatrics sports stadium where a huge billboard said, 'Annual Team Trials Today. Come and see if *you've* got what it takes to be a real Geriatric.' A little bunch of hopefuls in track suits were frozen in the act of filing in through the gate.

Trafalgar glared at the sign. He remembered these trials all too well. These were the famous trials at which Gravesend Geriatrics had found their amazing star player, Tito. All at once he was hit by the most awful thought. Far from being set to live happily ever after with Anya, he suddenly realised his problems were only just beginning. He already knew as an immutable fact that Anya was set to go off with the man. Both he and Stilts had seen it, after all, when she'd kissed him after the match. He stopped in his tracks and gave a little sob.

'Come on,' said Stilts. 'What's wrong? Don't stand still. People might see you.'

'It's no good,' said Trafalgar. 'I've just realised. She's bound to leave me too.'

'Anya? Why?'

No, said Trafalgar to himself, this is not the way the new Trafalgar behaves. The new Trafalgar sorts things out. The new Trafalgar would go in there right now and make quite sure no whippersnapper upstart would be selected in the trials. He would nip it in the bud. I'll find him, he thought. I'll find him and I'll keep tripping him up if I have to. He'll never know what hit him.

He stormed out onto the pitch and glared at the crowd of young hopefuls who were being put through their paces with the golf carts, the mallets and the balls. None of them looked remotely likely to be Tito. He went back to the sidelines and marched along furiously, staring at the ground, trying to decide what to do.

Back in Anya's apartment, there was a sudden sparking inside the remains of the keyboard and a faint smell of burning insulation.

Trafalgar suddenly noticed that the grass was turning from red to green. Noise started up again all around him. He looked up and saw that the statues out on the pitch had begun to move again. They were running, but with no great speed. One of them was clearly better than all the rest, a man with a helmet on – a man wearing the number twenty-three shirt. The grass might be green but Trafalgar saw red.

Afterwards, the Geriatrics coach and all the staff tended to disagree on the fine details of what they'd seen but more or less agreed on the main points. A tall man dressed in his ordinary clothes had suddenly come rushing on to the pitch at a speed none of them had ever witnessed before, had tackled their best player, Senta Forwood, sent him flying simply by the speed of his interception and had then kicked the ball so hard that it glowed red then exploded in midair from the heat build-up caused by air friction.

They moved forward as one to sign him up.

'What's your name, son?' said the coach.

Trafalgar was about to say 'Trafalgar Hurlock' when it struck him that this was a very bad idea with another Trafalgar Hurlock currently in circulation. Just then someone else elbowed his way very fast through the scrum surrounding him.

'His name's T2,' said the man in a fast, high-pitched voice.

'Who the hell are you?' said the coach.

'My name's S2,' said Stilts. 'I'm his manager.'

'Tito and Esto,' said the coach. 'I got it. Glad to meet you, guys.' He stuck out a hand, then shook it vigorously with a startled yelp as Trafalgar tried to shake it as gently as he could.

Back at the apartment, Stilts took a good look at the machine. 'Thought so,' he said. 'The oscillator's failed. It's stuck on the default time fast-forward setting. That gives us about twenty per cent extra speed whenever it's switched on.'

'Is that enough?'

'Enough to make you a sporting legend,' said Stilts. 'Enough to make us a decent living while we wait to catch up with our lives. Enough to retire in comfort after a short and glorious sporting career and enough to make sure that when Anya takes up with Tito, she's showing her complete loyalty to you in the nicest possible way.'

Trafalgar stretched out in an armchair and smiled. 'You know,' he said, 'for the first time, I really feel we've got this whole time travel business sorted out nicely.'

There was a sudden fizzing noise and a wisp of smoke. Two tiny and unfamiliar figures appeared. They were less than half Trafalgar's height and dressed in outlandish clothes.

'Trafalgar Hurlock and Stilton Cheesemaker?' one of them piped in a tiny high-pitched voice.

'Er, yes?' said Trafalgar, startled.

'You are summoned to appear before the northern hemispheric magistrate's court, traffic violations subsection at 11 am on August 14th, 3190 SEGES on a hundred and eighty-two charges of unlicensed use of a time vehicle, violations of the chrononavigational code of conduct and reckless tampering with the proper chain of events.'

'SEGES?' asked Trafalgar faintly.

'Since everything got even smaller,' said the figure, handing him a writ and disappearing in a tiny cloud of smoke.

240